Cover Copy

To love and protect…across worlds.

On planet Magio war rages between Peacio's protectors and Dralion's warriors. Friendships and soul-bonds are forbidden, yet deadly secrets lurk within a high-ranking inner circle.

Peacio's Silvie Carver is attempting to complete her finals when her best friend receives forewarning that she's the key to keeping her enemy king from making a decision that will escalate the war. Silvie must save her loved ones' soul-bonds from being torn apart, and all without revealing her emerging and rare fire skill during the mission.

Dralion warrior and enchanter, Guy Moyer, has been fighting his soul's demand to find his mated one...who also happens to be his enemy. Except Silvie shows up on Dralion's off-world Australian Outback station and though they renounce their bond, his soul demands he aid and protect her.

When Silvie finds herself impersonating a warrior, she's pulled to the fiery edge of her control as she seeks to influence the king's decision. Can the mated pair turn the tide of the war and find their place with each other?

Books by Joanne Wadsworth

Books by Joanne Wadsworth

ENCHANTER

Princesses of Myth, Book Three

JOANNE WADSWORTH

Enchanter
ISBN-13: 978-1-99-003417-6
Copyright © 2014, Joanne Wadsworth
Cover Art by Joanne Wadsworth
First electronic publication: May 2014

Joanne Wadsworth
http://www.joannewadsworth.com

AUTHOR'S NOTE:
This book is a work of fiction. The names, characters, places, and incidents are products of the writer's imagination or have been used fictitiously and are not to be construed as real. Any resemblance to persons, living or dead, actual events, locale or organizations is entirely coincidental. The author does not have any control over and does not assume any responsibility for third-party websites or their content.

Published in the United States of America

First digital publication: May 2014
First print publication: May 2014

Dedication

For my son, Cruise, who amazes me with his ability to invent and discover. You are so precious. Hugs.

Acknowledgements

I have the best family, and huge thanks go to my hubby, Jason, and kiddies, Marisa, Caleb, Cruise and Rocco. I love your smiles, and for giving me tons of time to write.

To my amazing editor, Penny Barber. You're so dedicated, and I'm one of the luckiest authors to have you.

For my readers, this series lives because you joined me, taking the journey to where imagination and magic soar. If you can dream it, you can do it.

And here's to another dream of mine, to Silvie and Guy's story. I've been longing to share this one with you.

Chapter 1

Unbelievable. My best friend had some nerve. Sprinting down the edge of the football field, I had to get away from my urge to crush Faith like the dry grass beneath my sneakers. I dodged the running back with eyes only for the rugby ball and hoped he'd slow Faith enough for me to get away.

"Silvie Carver, slow down," Faith yelled.

"You have forethought. You should have seen this coming."

"I didn't know you'd get this angry."

"I didn't know you'd dump this kind of news on me."

Chasing me, she ducked and dodged around the team. "Your temper should come with a warning."

"I'm a redhead. Get used to it." Ha! Faith's forethought was what needed a warning.

"Okay, so I shouldn't have just blurted out my problem."

"Ya think?" I made a beeline for the far gate.

"Let me try this again. It's not like my forewarning has happened yet."

"But it's going to." She was gaining on me, had hardly lost a breath, while I panted madly.

"Damn right it is. My skill is so freakin' annoying. Flaring up all over the place, and at the worst times."

"Your king is a tyrant. I have my own king and country to

worry about. I want nothing to do with yours or Dralion. Nothing."

"Best friends forever, Silvie. He's my grandfather and I need your help to figure this all out."

Now I had the stitch. It shot down one side. Skidding to a stop, I clutched my ribs. "Ugh, I really need to get more exercise."

Faith whizzed past then jogged back. "Thank you. I just need you to listen."

"I'm not listening. I'm unfit, if you didn't notice." It was alright for her, being so highly skilled and all. She ran every morning at dawn just to get rid of her excess energy. Me, I snoozed. No use rolling out of bed until absolutely necessary.

"I'm really sorry about this coming disaster."

"The disaster is Donaldo Wincrest." Heck, saying his name out loud was enough to set me off. "I can't stand him. Your grandfather's always sending his warriors onto Peacio's shores, with my people in the firing line."

"We can't choose who we're related to."

"It'd make life a lot easier if we could." Bummer, though, that she'd found out she was a Wincrest. Eighteen years and she'd never known.

"At least we can choose who our best friends are, and you're mine."

"Geez, I hate your forewarnings. Why can't we just have a regular school day? Death and disaster should be off limits."

"My forewarnings don't work that way." She squeezed my shoulder. "My father is the last person any of us expected him to be, but I love him and I'm dealing with the cards dealt."

"I'm dealing too, but not if it involves Dralion."

"C'mon, pleazzze."

I didn't dare look into her eyes. Those stupid pleases of hers niggled at my heart and got me every time. "My king sent me to Earth to watch over you when we were kids, not your newfound family. Carlisio Loveria wouldn't appreciate it if I ended up getting my nose stuck in the enemy's business."

"I can't ask anyone else." She tweaked my chin. "Hey, you've gotta look at me."

"No." Her voice was pitched just right too, making my "no" not nearly strong enough.

"You're a sister to me, and Magio is all so new."

Damn. Not the sister card. Stand strong. Don't fold.

"Silvie, the battle between our nations, and the fact I have a mate I can't speak about, is difficult, but at least I have you. We've always stuck together."

"I can't go against my country. Ask your mate for help. Davio loves slashing his sword around. Just mention Wincrest's name, and my cousin's your man."

"I can't tell Davio about my vision." She paced in front of me, clutching the sides of her denim miniskirt. "I've already used my forethought and factored him into the problem. The results weren't pretty. He's one totally obstinate prince. I need you, not my mate."

"Yours and Davio's relationship is strong. He got over who you were related to. Give him more credit."

"I do, but we have to take such care." She squeezed her eyes shut. "I can't work through this forewarning without you. This fight isn't mine, yet I've been dropped into the middle of it."

And it appeared, so had I. So not fair when I couldn't keep ignoring her plea. We'd grown up together and always had each other's back. "Argh, okay, give me some more information so at least I can think about it."

"Is that a yes? We stick together?"

"It's give me more information."

"You won't regret this."

"I'm sure I will."

"Right." The wind blew her long blond hair about her face.

She flicked it away. "So I got to the part before about Donaldo being involved."

"Yeah, your tyrannical king who knows how to throw everything into chaos."

"Just try to put your frustrations aside."

I breathed deep, instilling some calm for Faith's sake. Discovering her father was Dralion's Prince Alexo when he'd returned to Earth for her and her mother had been difficult, but it hadn't destroyed our friendship. Our eighteen years together counted. "Okay, I'll try."

"What happens, is Donaldo makes an announcement soon. One which involves Hope too. Heck, I still can't believe I have an identical twin sister. It's just as well our blood-bond cemented the moment we came together." She blew out a long breath, as if needing a moment to calm herself. "Okay, so saying yes to me, is saying yes to her. We both need your help."

"How is Hope involved?" I adored my brother's new mate. I had to keep her safe.

"My forewarning affects so many people if I don't get it sorted. Hope and Silas. Davio and me. We're just the beginning."

"Grrreat." With all four of my closest involved, I barely had a choice. "Lay the rest of the details on me, and be gentle. Gentle."

"Hope and I are in Donaldo's grand dining room." Sweat popped up along her brow and she wiped it away. "There's a formal dinner and the leading eight are seated."

"Dralion's elite fighting force, right?"

"Yes."

"Lovely." Not only was her king involved, but the fiercest of the fierce. How could she possibly think I could help? I had no skills. "Your forewarning was bad enough with Donaldo in it. Now you're adding the leading eight?"

"Only two of them, Killian and Abelard."

"Oh, only two." Sheesh. "That's so much better then."

"You ready for more?"

"No."

"Killian makes his demand clear, that he's there to court me. Abelard rises and states his desire to court Hope, except a lot more brutally than what I just said. Things get pretty heated."

"Holy moly. Do I even want to know what happens next?" I didn't, except best friends didn't let each other down. "No. Don't answer that. Just tell me."

"My skill doesn't work on me, and my forewarning kept blurring because I couldn't keep my focus from myself. Then when I finally shoved it back on Hope so I could get some clarity, Donaldo stood and boomed his agreement. Killian and Abelard are slayers." Her face paled. "They kill the enemy just for the sheer pleasure of it."

"Wincrest is such a dictator."

"Davio and Silas—" She gulped. "The war between our nations already rages. Hope and I want to see peace prevail. I can't have this problem added to it."

"Hold on. You're only eighteen. Why would Wincrest agree to a courtship this soon?"

"No one knows Hope and I have mates, and it's not like we can spill the news. My guess is we're fair game in Killian and Abelard's eyes."

"What about your father or aunt? Can't they help?" Alexo and Goldie were loyal to Wincrest, but they also revered the bond. Alexo had lived without his wife for eighteen years, fearing Wincrest would find and remove her. He'd never inflict the same pain on his daughters. It was probably his only redeeming quality, in my eyes.

"Nothing changed when I factored them into my forewarning, yet the moment I did with you, bingo, the forewarning dissolved. Somehow, you're the key. It's you who has the ability to halt what's about to happen."

"How am I the key?" I wobbled, and she propped an arm under my shoulder.

"You're the last person I want dragged into Dralion's business, but I can't prevent what's about to happen, and it seems no one else can, other than you." She shuddered. "I don't want Killian courting me, not when I'm mated to Davio. My soul is bound to his, and I'd never survive losing him."

"Okay, but you've gotta give me more than 'I'm the key.'"

"That's not how my forewarning works. It's you who figures out a resolution. I can only say you're the one who discovers it."

"I seriously, seriously hate your skill." A student dashed past us, nabbed his bike from the bike bay and rode through the gate.

"Every decision we make can alter the course of our future. It's always in flux, but to fix what's coming, I need you. Please." She squeezed my arm. "Let's work together."

I couldn't let Faith down, not with this massive problem on the horizon. Even with Dralion involved, I had to do what I could. "Hope has to be brought into the loop. I can't leave her out of this since your forewarning involves both of you."

"I don't want to leave her out of it either. I'll take you to her in the outback, but you'll have to keep a low profile. Warriors 'port in and out of Wincrest Station." The station was one of Dralion's off-world ventures. Faith had been raised here in New Zealand with her mother, and Hope in both Dralion and their Australian holding.

"That's all right. I'll simply be your friend from Earth."

"That'll work. Let me check exactly where she is." Her eyes glazed as she focused with her forethought. It was such a rare skill, one only held by the two ruling families of Magio. It was also the skill which had begun our world's war a thousand years ago, and still wreaked havoc today. "Found her. She's in the yard near the corral."

"So, we're good to go?"

"Yes, I'll 'port us from behind one of the furthest trees." Her gaze cleared, and the deep Wincrest violet denoting her strong line shone through.

"Sounds good." The coach blew his whistle and the football team jogged to the bright blue changing rooms off the gym. Most of the students had gone home, and only a few stragglers remained near the bus bay. "On a brighter note, I've always wanted to visit the outback."

"I doubt you wanted to visit it like this."

"Try never, but I can deal."

"That's why I love you, Silvie."

"Oh, so now you're trying to butter me up?"

"Yep." She tugged me to the tree she favored with its wide trunk. "Because the place is in drought, and it's hot enough to melt the soles of your shoes if you stand in one place for too long."

"Don't worry. I love a hot day." I squeezed her hand. "I'll be careful."

"You're the best friend I could ever have." She hugged me, and then everything darkened as she 'ported us, as she made the jump through time and space.

We arrived in the blinding sunshine. Oh yeah. Heat. Beautiful.

"Wow, it's hotter than hot." She fanned her face. "Do you see Hope? She was right here."

"Not yet." I peered between the wooden beamed rails of the horse corral. A stallion pranced within, kicking up red dust as he snorted. "She's not in there, and that horse looks ready to bolt."

"Maybe she went to get him something. If she did, she'll be that way." She tilted her head toward a long run of white weatherboard stables.

Following her, I jammed one loose tail of my red t-shirt into my denim cutoffs. At least my Earth clothing should pass initial inspection. Warriors usually wore battle leathers, the same as my country's elite protectors. "Donaldo Wincrest never comes here, right?"

"You're safe. It's just Goldie and Hope who run this place. They were raised together and spent half their lives here."

We stepped through the open doors and into a wide central holding room. On one wall, hooks held saddles and tack. I stroked one of the long reins, polished to perfection. On the opposite wall, square bales of hay had been stacked to the ceiling, a dozen high and a good twenty bales wide. Hmm, nothing here so far to worry—nope. At the back of the stables, perched on a wooden stool before a workbench, a man gripped a silver stirrup which glowed red on one end. He was heating the object, and without fire.

A warrior. He must be one of Dralion's highly skilled.

Someone from Peacio would be dubious, but I had to act the part of an Earthling. I couldn't show any fear. I stepped closer.

Black hair fell forward over his brow, his hair so silky it shone midnight blue on the ends.

He jerked around, his gaze landing on me.

I kept my composure. "Hey."

"Who are you?" He stood, his impressive height a good hand over six feet. He would tower over me by a foot. I should be intimidated, but oh, what broad shoulders. His white shirt stretched tight over his chest, and dark leather pants cupped his butt to perfection. His sword, belted low on his right hip, brushed the dusty floorboards.

What? Why was I ogling the enemy? Get it together.

"Ah, I'm Silvie, a friend of Faith's." His eyes were to die for. Silver swirled around the edges of his pale blue eyes, the stunning metallic color displaying his strongly skilled line. An enchanter.

"No! This can't be happening." He gripped the hilt of his

sword, and his nostrils flared. "You should never have come."

"What do you mean?"

"Guy, it's fine. I brought Silvie, and it was important she come." Faith held up a hand. "I'm after Hope. Did she come in here?"

"Yes. She's down the corridor. One of the mares is in labor and she ran to check on her. Go, but be quiet." He set the stirrup on his workbench, and the melted end oozed into a metallic puddle.

"How'd you melt that?" What he'd done was enthralling.

"It's the spell of heat without fire. What's your last name, Silvie?" His gaze traveled over me, not missing an inch. Strangely, I enjoyed it. Hold on. What was wrong with me? He was still a warrior.

"Carver," Faith interrupted. "Guy, she's in the know, like you are." The girls had a tight inner circle of those they trusted. And since Guy kept Faith and Hope's secret as I did, he had to be one of the few good ones. I must have sensed that. Somehow.

"Right." He snorted then turned back to his workbench. "Take her away, Faith."

"Come on." Faith tugged my hand.

"No, I'd like to stay and get to know one of the warriors you trust so much. Go and find Hope. I'll wait." He completely intrigued me.

"You sure? He doesn't sound like he wants you here."

"If he's in the know, then I'm safe. Just go." I studied the warrior as he whispered a spell over the stirrup he'd set down.

"Okay, I'll be as quick as I can." Faith dashed away.

"You should have gone with her." He cast me a sideways glance. "Carver, eh? Any relation to Hope's mate, the protector Silas?"

"Maybe." I advanced on him.

"You have the same blue eyes as Carver. Doesn't he have a twin sister? One I've heard is close to Faith?" He slowly circled me. "Yeah, you're her."

"What's your last name?"

His gaze flickered with frustration as he came nose to nose. "Moyer."

My heartbeat thumped at his closeness. "The son of Gerritt, and the grandson of Gilles?"

"You've heard of my line?"

"Everyone has. Forty years ago, Gilles Moyer spelled the dome's energy field into existence over Dralion." Which meant this man was from one of Dralion's strongest enchanting lines. Although, not the wisest since his father had been captured at the battle of Eventide two years ago and now resided within Peacio's containment cells. A heavy weight settled in my chest and I couldn't stop myself from touching his hand. "I'm sorry for your loss, your father." Boy, why did I feel such a sudden connection with him?

"He still lives, and soon he'll be freed. I'll see to it." He clamped his hand over mine. The silver in his eyes swirled to life, as if he were about to spell.

"Don't even try it. I may be unskilled, but I'm tough."

"There's a spell which turns back time." He tightened his grip on me. "We should never have met. Don't you feel it?"

Inside me an urge to be even nearer burned, and I was quite close enough.

"The bond." He threaded our fingers together. "You're my mated one, and damn it. This shouldn't be happening."

Oh my goodness. The truth blazed in his eyes. That's what this was. I'd never in my life felt an attraction to any man. Sure, I'd had plenty of male friends, but none had ever stirred me the way Guy had from the moment I'd seen him. We were mated, the soul-bond pulsing to life between us.

Crap.

I was mated to a warrior. Only half our people were soul-bound. "What do we do?"

He fisted his hands at his sides. "At times I've felt the male's drive within the bond toward Earth, and at other times Magio. I expected my mated one was a Peacian since it's only your people who have the freedom to travel. It's why I stayed away."

"So you decided to let our bond pass?"

"There's a war, and we'd never suit. Wouldn't you do the same?"

"I would have wanted to know, so at least"—I fluttered my fingers between us—"I could move on."

"You're a friend of the girls. It isn't going to be easy to move on."

"Our meeting doesn't have to change anything. I go to school in New Zealand and that's a long way from here. Same with Peacio."

"Then I doubt our paths will cross." He rubbed his thumb along his chin. The cleft in the center added to his intense look. "Why would you go to an Earth school if you're a Peacian?"

"I was charged with keeping an eye on Faith a very long time ago. I'm also attending culinary school there next year."

"You favor the art of cooking?" He frowned. "My mother did too, before she passed. She made everything, from the bread each morning to the Sunday roast dripping in gravy. I was only small, but I'd pull up a stool to stand on and help her peel the vegetables." He slowly reached out and caught a length of my hair. Gently, he wrapped one lock around his finger.

"I'm so sorry about your mother, Guy." I scraped one foot forward, touching my toe to his, needing some form of connection too.

"She had the biggest heart, the gentlest smile, and hair as black as midnight, so long it touched her waist, right about"—he smoothed down my sides and cupped my hips—"here."

Heat raced through my veins and I shuffled my other foot forward. Closer was better, and no doubt due to the bond at play.

"You miss her?"

"Always." He slid his thumbs into the small gap between the waistband of my cutoffs and t-shirt. "She was life itself, which is why I appreciate the here and now. You never know when someone will be gone."

My chest tightened, his loss cutting into me far more than it should. "She sounds wonderful."

"She was." He pulled back a little and fingered his necklace. From the center of the thin strap of leather, a small gold ring dangled. "It's been so long. I almost forgot. My mother bequeathed her ring to my mated one. She gave it to me to hold onto until the time we met."

"What? No. We might be mated, but we're not doing anything about it, right?"

"Right." He lifted the necklace free of his head. "But I still made a promise."

"No, really." I shoved against his chest. "Stop. Put that back on. Promises like that can be broken."

"Not this one. My mother wanted the woman I was mated with to know her in some way. This ring was her gift to you. I'm only the keeper, passing it along."

I backed up until my shoulders knocked the hay bales. "I said stop."

"Her wishes were precise." He crowded me from the front, making it impossible to get away, and then slipped the necklace over my head. "This was what my mother wanted. It feels good to see to her last request. Don't deny me that."

Nothing could have shocked me more. Off balance, I rocked onto my heels, gripping the band of gold, his mother's precious gift from the past. "This is crazy."

"I'll know you have it. That's all that matters." Guy's brow pulled down as he clasped my hand. "We really should end things now, before our soul-bond deepens further."

"You mean release each other?"

"Exactly. I'm the last enchanter in my line, and even though I'm only nineteen, Donaldo has already requested I find a warrior woman and continue it. I have to ensure the ability to enchant doesn't die away with me."

Damn, this was all happening so fast. "Shouldn't we take some time before we decide on such a step?"

"My destiny is not with you, Silvie. It's elsewhere."

"For eighteen years I've dreamed of being mated."

"We can't move on until we release each other."

The heaviness in my chest expanded. Geez, what a predicament. This was the right thing to do, even though it felt totally wrong.

"Don't think too much about it." He caught my face between his hands. "Just start. Speak the words I need to hear."

"You're this certain?"

"Yes. I'm sorry." His voice scraped on the last word, as if he fought his emotions.

I could do this. I was strong, and surely didn't need a warrior for a mate. I'd already seen how hard it was for Faith and Hope, and now, the future difficulties they faced. That wasn't for me.

"Give me a second." I wet my suddenly dry lips then forced them open. "Guy, I wish for you to find the right woman, to have a long and wonderful life with her." Uh-huh, a good start. "That you'll have the family you desire, and of course, that she be anyone other than me."

"Thank you." He kissed my cheek. "Silvie, I wish to release you, so you might find the right man. I wish for him to keep you safe and to cherish you, to give you all you desire, and…be anyone other than me."

Tears welled in my eyes and I shoved them back. I would not cry over him.

"Do you want a breather?"

"Yes."

"I'll go wait outside until Faith returns. We did the right thing."

"I know." I slipped his mother's ring under the neckline of my t-shirt as he strode away. I'd keep it safe, just as I would the other half of his soul, even though he was no longer mine.

A tear leaked past my guard and I swiped it away. Stupid bond, and I couldn't stop myself from following him. I gripped the splintered edge of the doorway to halt my step. "Don't go too far. This is Wincrest Station."

"There're no other warriors about. You're safe." He climbed the railing, and then cautiously approached the prancing stallion within. Gently, he cooed its name.

"Hey, Silvie." Hope strolled in from the corridor in jeans and a red-checked outback shirt, Faith one step behind her. She wiped her hands on a raggedy towel hanging from her pocket.

"Hey back at ya. How's the mare?"

"One very contented new mama. The foal is a little wobbly, but already up on her legs."

Faith grinned at me. "It was incredible to watch the birth. A-maz-ing." She glanced about the room and frowned. "Ah, where's Guy?"

"Outside." The sun bathed him in its brightness, and I couldn't keep my gaze from him.

She strode to the doorway and called out, "Hey, everything okay?"

"It will be." His scorching gaze narrowed on me as he fed the stallion a treat.

Faith jerked a look between the two of us. "Is there something going on here? I didn't leave you guys alone for long enough to cause too big a fight, did I?"

"We didn't fight, in fact we chatted, and then—" Oh, how to tell her? I shuffled from foot to foot, rucking up the dust.

"Then what?"

"Um, we released each other."

"Released each other?" Her eyebrows launched into her hairline. Yeah, for once I'd surprised her. Which with her forethought, was close to impossible. "No way. You two are mated?"

Hope darted a look at Guy. "This is unbelievable. You always sensed your mated one was a Peacian, but Silvie?"

"That's right." He scaled the railing and returned. "Now we've met though, we've ended things. It's as it should be."

"No, Guy." Faith shook her head, clearly not happy. "There's a reason our souls are bound. Perhaps you two just need some more time to talk." She glanced at Hope. "What do you think?"

"It can't hurt them."

"Great. Let's give them some space." She grabbed Hope's hand and flashed them away.

"What? Faith, no. You can't leave me here like that." Drat. How could she bail on me? Sure, she would hate I hadn't given this soul-bond a chance, particularly when she worked so hard on hers and Davio's relationship.

"They've gone, and don't worry about it. I'll take you home. Just tell me where that is."

"I should have guessed she'd do that. I'm so sorry."

"They care, although that doesn't change our decision." He seized my arm. "Where to?"

"Loveria Castle. That's where I live when I'm not on Earth. Except, make it the outer fields where there won't be any protectors." He couldn't be seen by the guards.

"Gotcha. I know exactly where."

The dark encompassed us, and then we were there.

He squinted at Loveria Castle looming high on the hill in the distance. "Is this far enough away?"

"It should be. How'd you know about this spot?" The protectors stationed in the twin-towered gatehouse lookout towers could see for miles, but a copse of pines shielded us.

"How'd you have an image to 'port us here?"

"Know the land of your enemy and all." Hands in his pockets, he watched wispy clouds float over the castle's massive gray stone walls. "I've been here a few times, Silvie."

"Enemy? I'm not personally yours. I never will be because of the bond."

"Broken bond." He touched his chest. "And I know."

"If you want to leave, then don't mind me. There's no need for us to talk like Faith said."

"You've nothing else you want to say?" The silver rimming his blue eyes dulled. Okay, not fair. He'd been the one to insist we release each other. I couldn't have him jerking on my heartstrings now. I had to toughen up if I was to get through this.

"Nope." I dusted my hands off on my legs. "Get going, pretty boy."

"Pretty boy?"

"Yep, we've already spoken our release, so you can go and find that nice warrior woman you're after." I turned on my heel. Walk. One step in front of the other. Don't stop. Still, my heart heaved with each step I took. Stupid heartstrings.

"That's it?" he called out.

"Sayonara."

"What the hell?"

"It means goodbye." I stomped through the thick grass, wishing it was his heart I tramped on and not mine. Uphill. Keep moving.

"You're angry?"

"Apparently it's the day for it."

A burst of air from behind whisked my hair into my face, and then his arm whipped around my waist. He tumbled me into him. "I can't leave if you're upset."

"I'm not upset, and I'm not yours to worry about. Go."

"Just like that?"

"Yes." I closed my eyes.

"This isn't right. Look at me." His fingertips skimmed my cheek.

"It'll be easier if you just go. Please." I needed to remain strong.

"Then take care, my mate." His thumb swept over my lower lip. "I wish you well."

His mate? No, he would be with someone else in the future.

I waited, struggling not to reach for him. Birds high in the forest of pines ceased chirping. His clothing rustled as he stepped away. A shift in the air caused the hairs on my arms to bristle. I opened my eyes. He was gone. His absence left a void, constricting my lungs and making me gasp for breath.

Unwanted tears rose and I gave in, letting them spill. Each drop would cleanse me.

My mate had never cared to truly know me.

Now he'd never return.

His loss, and mine.

Chapter 2

My chest still throbbed, made worse since I stood in my favorite place and couldn't lift a finger. I'd barely been able to sleep last night, but I had to soldier on. School loomed. At least yesterday was over. I never had to go through the pain of—nope. I wouldn't even say his name.

I tapped the bright red countertop, which matched the red kitchen cabinets trimmed with white. Princess Genevy, Davio's mother, had built this kitchen for me five years ago. I loved cooking, and my passion would see me through the days ahead. This space in this lower northern wing for us younger ones usually wrapped me in its warmth, but I didn't even want to peek through my cookbooks for inspiration today. I shuffled across the white slate floor and slumped overtop the cold metal sink. Out the white wooden edged window, the sun's rays beamed in over a thick green garden. My favorite herbs thrived there, but they didn't call to me to come and pillage. So much for my place of solace.

"Hey, Silvie."

The door swung open and Zayn ambled in. The protector with his tousled blond hair and sun-kissed skin appeared as if he belonged at the beach and surfing the waves instead of with a sword in hand and defending our borders. It was made even more obvious since he wore Earth clothing, a pair of tan cargo shorts and a striped t-shirt over his usual battle leathers.

From his top pocket, he pulled out a pair of sunglasses then slid them on. "Whatcha think? I've got the day off and I need to blend in with the New Zealand locals. I hardly ever take a look around. It's always a quick visit in and out."

"You look perfect. If you want, I'll even show you around." Having someone else to distract me today would help.

"Nah, you've got school. Silas sent me to take you this morning."

"I don't feel up to it." That was an understatement. Come on. Cheer up. Zayn was never in a dull mood, and he'd surely lift mine. "One day off isn't gonna hurt." I snagged his sunnies. "Where'd you get these? On one of those quick visits?" We lived in a society more like Earth's from a couple hundred centuries ago, and I'd never seen him wear such a thing.

"Travel's free. I shopped." He snatched them back. "And yeah, I'll take you up on your offer. I almost got run over by an SUV when I went to buy these. Boy, are those big brutes."

I laughed, and that lump in my chest lightened a little more. "You have to look both ways before you cross the blacktop."

"I will. Next time. It's a shame Earthlings can't 'port."

"You're just lucky you can." I prodded his chest. "So where's my brother? I haven't had a chance to tell him about yesterday." I always told him the big stuff, and he'd want to know I'd found my—yep, the nameless one. He'd want to know.

"He and Davio have already 'ported to Sunider. They're in the middle of running border checks between us and the desert area of No-Man's Land."

"Ah, that's right. I remember him mentioning that now." Faith and Hope had recently discovered their mother's lost heritage had come from the Sol desert tribe. Kate had been abandoned on Earth by her Magioling mother thirty-six years ago. She'd not known of this world until Alexo had come for her and Faith a few short months ago.

Davio and Silas were insistent the Sol's No-Man's Land location was safeguarded. They cared for their mates in all ways.

Hmm, mates. I patted Guy's mother's ring where it rested under the top edge of my red tank top. It was all I had of him, of the man who should have been mine. Argh, I had to stop these mushy thoughts. Get it together. He'd moved on. I'd moved on. I shoved my hands into the pockets of my shorts so I wouldn't touch the ring again. "I can't wait to have some fun. I so need it."

"Right, but after breakfast. Fun requires food." From inside the pantry, he grabbed a box of cereal then headed to the fridge. He stroked the metallic surface before opening it. "My mum has a cold-box, but nothing lasts in there for more than a day or two. She'd love this."

I snuck the jug of milk out. "She can't have it. This fridge is all mine."

"You're safe. I wouldn't pinch it, not when she likes making the younger ones run out to the cold-box so often." He pulled plates and glasses from the cupboard and spoons from the drawer.

"How many children are in your family?" He hardly ever spoke of them.

"Ten. I'm the eldest. I'm glad I don't live at home anymore."

"Ten?" Whoa, that many kids would keep her way busy. Poor woman. "Your mum must be run off her feet. I have a new recipe for lasagna I'd intended to cook this afternoon. I'll make it for her if she'd like it." It'd keep me busy too, and I so needed that.

"She'd love it. Let me 'path her." He took all of ten seconds as he did. "It's a resounding yes, but you'll have to come if you're making dinner. I'll go too. She won't accept anything else." With his hands full, he knocked his backside into the swing door leading to the dining room and opened it. "Coming?"

He kept it open with one foot.

"Yes, to both offers."

A wide grin slashed his face. "No, thank you. The least I can do is open the door if you're cooking dinner tonight." He let the door swing shut after I walked through.

I straightened the silver threaded tablecloth covering the long oak dining table. Through the wide bay window adorned with silver-edged emerald curtains, the iron gates of the gatehouse rolled open. Protectors rode out on horseback toward the river where Guy had dropped me off. To think he knew of that spot, had watched the castle from that close. How many times had that happened? And when? The male felt the drive to seek out his bonded mate when she received her skills on her eighteenth. Even though unskilled, my eighteenth had passed a few months ago.

"Silvie?" Zayn held out my chair. "You look a little lost, like you were when I first saw you in the kitchen. Is something up?"

I sat and poured cereal into my bowl. Zayn was a trusted member of our inner circle. Anything I told him would remain between us, and it appeared I couldn't lighten this dark mood. "I met someone yesterday, well more than someone."

"Who's that?" He poured my milk then nudged a spoon toward me.

"Guy Moyer, a warrior." I shoved a spoonful of cereal into my mouth.

"You met a warrior?"

"He's my mate, although we released each other."

"I've heard of him." He drummed his fingers on the tabletop. "He's the last remaining enchanter in the Moyer line. Are you all right? That had to have been hard."

"Even though I barely spent any time with him, he got under my skin." I shoveled more food into my mouth. My chest tightened with each mention of Guy's name.

"It must have been difficult." He resumed eating. "I've told so very few about this, but on my eighteenth, I felt the urge to find my soul-bound one."

What? He was mated? No way. "You've never said. Why not?"

"Because the direction of that drive leads toward Dralion."

"Damn. I'm so sorry." My heart lost a beat as his words sank in. "So, you understand how I'm feeling?"

He squeezed my hand. "More than you could ever know. It's a bond I'll never be able to embrace, and the finality of that is a burden I can barely stand. If you ever need to speak of what you're feeling, then I'm here. I usually make a great listener."

"How do you deal with it? I've at least met my mate and given our relationship closure."

"I don't have a choice. It can never be, and the dome ensures it."

"Yeah, the dome sucks. Thanks for understanding."

"You're not alone. Half our people remain unmated, and I'm certain their bound one is beyond their reach. So many don't speak of it. What's Moyer like?"

"He cares about Faith and Hope, although he was quick to tell me we wouldn't work out. So I guess, honest. I met him in the outback."

"Wincrest Station?"

"Yep."

"Which means you may come across him again since he's close to the girls. They are his princesses."

"I think we'll manage to keep our distance from each other." My stomach churned, and I shoved my plate away. I didn't want to keep my distance from him, but I'd get past this. As time moved on, it'd get easier, or at least, it better. "Since we're playing hooky, we have to hit the beach."

"Sold." Pushing away from the table, he grinned. "Papamoa beach sound good?"

"Perfect." I gripped his arm. "Lead the way, my chauffeur."

He chuckled as he 'ported us, and then we arrived, our feet sinking into the glorious white sands of my favorite beach. What a perfect spot for tossing out a towel, lying back and lapping up the sun's gorgeous rays.

"We are sooo gonna have some fun today." I shielded my eyes from the glare. Surfers rode the farthest breakers of the mighty Pacific Ocean, and seagulls squawked and circled for fish. White capped waves tumbled in and surged to our feet. I darted back, keeping my toes dry.

The surf hit Zayn's legs and sprayed over his shorts. "Ahh, now that's what I'm after." He stripped his shirt over his head and wrapped his sunnies inside before lobbing the bundle toward the dunes. "Are you coming in?"

"I'm not a fan of cold water. I'm here for the sun, but you have fun out there."

"Will do." He ran into the waves, let out a whoop then dived.

Oh, this was the way to have a day off. The wind coming off the ocean whipped my hair about my face, and I raised my hands to the sky and soaked in the warm sunshine. Purrrfect.

Such peace after the turbulence of yesterday.

Hmm, except for the girls' problem. I should have been giving it my full attention. Only what on earth did I do to prevent Wincrest from allowing two of the leading eight to court the girls? I dug my feet into the sand. Oh yeah, the heated grains cocooned my toes and sent a tingle of pleasure through me.

"Silvie?" Guy's voice rumbled from close behind. "I know I shouldn't have come, but there's a problem."

My heartbeat thundered as I whipped around. Oh boy. It really was him. My mate stood before me when I'd never believed I'd see him again, and not fair, looking smokin' hot as well. Yum. Whoa. Eyes up. Get it together. "Ah, what kind of difficulty?"

"Faith told me why she brought you to the outback. The moment she factored you into her forewarning, it dissolved. She told me you're the key, except since you and I ended things"—he shoved one hand into his hair and tossed his silky black locks about—"she had another."

"Forewarning?" Oh no. Faith had far too many of those, and I hadn't sorted the current forewarning yet.

"Yeah. She's now factored me into it, and I hate to tell you this, but it appears I somehow aid you in being the key." The wind rushed along the beach, plastering his shimmery gray shirt against his wide chest.

"Aid?" He couldn't be serious. The task would be hard enough as it was without the distraction of him. Oh, and talk about toned abs. His silk shirt coated each defined dip. See, distraction. I planted my hands on my hips and forced my mind back on track. "As in assisting me? Together?"

"Not together, together. But definitely the two of us working as a team."

"I can't believe this." Faith better not be playing with me. Although, my best friend knew I'd never stand for any lies between us. Damn it, she really must have had another forewarning. "So, you're saying our relationship is still done? Finished?" I had to know what I'd be taking on if I accepted his help.

"Yes. Nothing changes. For the girls' sake, do you think we can work together on this problem?"

"If Faith says it's necessary, then of course. I don't like it, but I can handle it." Provided he covered that impressive chest with something less flimsy than that shirt. A jacket would be good. I should make that a stipulation he wear one. "Can you handle it?"

"If I—" His gaze slid over my shoulder and narrowed in on Zayn as he body-surfed the waves toward us. "Who's that? And why aren't you at school?"

"I'm on a date."

"Already?" He thumped his thighs covered in black rawhide pants. "With him?"

"Yes."

He snarled, and I jerked back. Okay, he wasn't allowed to get territorial. I'd have to make that a stipulation too. "Mated ones cannot speak a mistruth, Silvie. I can sense your lie."

Drat. I should have known he'd pick up on the lie. "So it's not exactly a date, but I needed someone to talk to, and Zayn was there. He knows about us. He's a protector." And why was I defending my actions? He'd given up the right to question me.

"You should have spoken to Faith or Hope, not him."

"They weren't there, and Zayn's trustworthy. He knows about them too."

"Next time speak to me. You're my mate." His pale blue eyes rimmed with silver narrowed.

"Yes, your mate. But one who you released."

"We're still soul-bound, and now working together. You can come to me until the girls' problem is sorted."

"No thanks. You said nothing's changed between us." I patted his chest, and a sizzle of heat scorched my fingertips. Well, apart from that. I really liked touching him.

"That doesn't mean—hell." He caught my hand and held it tight. "I'm sorry, this is a strange situation. I'll get some control and stop making demands. I shouldn't have overstepped my mark."

"Thank you. I'd appreciate that." My pulse sped, and I couldn't stop myself from wriggling closer. "How's your day been? 'Cause mine's been crappy."

"The pits. I didn't know it would be this hard."

With my free hand, I tip-toed my fingers across his chest. "Well, we can be moody together, if you like?"

"Silvie, stop that. It's dangerous." Heat pulsed from him.

"I like danger." I glanced at his mouth. What would it be

like to kiss him?

"No." His voice was raspy and hard. Oh yeah, I liked. "I can see what you're thinking. You're doubling the danger."

No doubt I was, but his being here wasn't helping either. "Why don't you leave then? No matter what Faith said, I can figure out the girls' problem without any help. We don't have to put ourselves through this turmoil."

"She was insistent, and I can't let her or Hope down. I gave my allegiance to my king and country. They're my princesses." Slowly, he reached out and touched his mother's ring swinging freely over my top. He pushed his little finger through the hole and slid it halfway on. "Mum had the tiniest fingers."

I slid my pinky finger around his, knuckle to knuckle with the gold band warm between us. "If you want the ring back, you only have to ask."

"No, it's yours." He stared into my eyes, and I wanted to drown in the soulful depths. "I'll never forget the moment she gave it to me. She was so sick toward the end. The healers said there was nothing they could do about her sickness. It had come too fast."

"I promise I'll keep it safe."

"Thank you." With a groan, he slipped his finger free.

"You don't have to stick around. It's probably best you don't."

"I know." He pointed at Zayn. "You need to ditch him. I'd feel more comfortable."

"Nope. I need to ditch you." Making the first move, I backed away, headed toward Zayn and waved.

He swam in and jogged over. "Who's that?"

"Guy Moyer."

"Ahh, I see." He shook his shirt free of sand then yanked it over his head and plopped his sunnies on.

"He just wanted to make sure I was okay after we ended things. I said I was." Best not to spill on Faith's problem. Zayn was too close to Davio and Silas and might say something.

"Right, and since he's not leaving, how about you introduce us?" He took my elbow. "And preferably before he comes over here and knocks my head off. That's one dark scowl he has."

Guy shoved his long sleeves to his elbows and met us half way. Double daggers sheathed at his wrists glinted in the sunshine. "Take your hands off her."

"You ended things." Zayn flexed his hand then smoothed it down his thigh, right where his sword normally lay. "But nice of you to check on her, not that it was necessary. You can be assured we protectors look after our own."

"It's been a while since I've enjoyed a good fight. Silas was the last protector I had some fun with."

I edged between them. "Just stop this now. I have enough to deal with, and I don't need you two coming head to head."

"We hadn't finished speaking. Excuse us." Guy glared at Zayn as he backed away and took me with him.

Good grief. Talk about an overabundance of male bonded drive. "What are you doing?"

"I have no idea, except I need to control these impulses you've fired in me. We'll begin working on the girls' problem this evening. You okay with that?"

"I can't do it this evening."

"Tomorrow night then?"

"Yes." I forced a step back then shooed him away. "Off you go."

"You're not to date another while we work together, and that's final." He shimmered and disappeared.

Argh, us working together wasn't Faith's best idea, but since we had to, we'd simply keep it to a minimum. Only, drat, I wished him right back again.

Zayn joined me. "Are you all right?"

"I will be. Thanks for asking." I squeezed his arm.

He jumped back and gawked at where I'd touched him.

"You just—" My fingerprints were burnt into his skin. "Unbelievable."

"Did I do that?" I had to be seeing things, only the evidence was clear. My handprint branded his arm.

"You just burnt me." He traced the marks, although they slowly faded as his fast-healing kicked in. He shot me a look. "We have to try that again."

I backed away but he advanced and gripped my arm before I could stop him.

"Shoot. Hot. Hot. Hot." Blisters, red and angry, bloomed on his fingertips.

"No more trying. I'm clearly burning you." His festered skin meant I'd come into a skill. "My Carver ancestors had the fire skill."

"It's been a couple of months since your eighteenth, but you and Silas were born prematurely."

"By seven weeks, but Silas still came into his skills the week of his eighteenth." Yeah, except Silas had been born healthy and strong, and me so tiny. It had taken months for me to catch up.

"Well, you definitely have a skill, and now there's a wicked amount of heat pulsing off you."

"There is?" Of course there would be. I'd just burnt him. "Stay there then. I don't want to burn you any more than I have." In awe, I grazed my fingers over my arm. "I have the fire skill. Wow."

"A skill with a high temperature. You're gonna have to get that down."

"I wouldn't have a clue how to. How much heat am I emitting? I can't sense it."

"A ton of it. Look, Belle's a wizard with tracking information on our skills. She knows the castle library inside out and that's where the facts about your fire skill will be. I'll 'path her and ask her to meet us there. We'll get some answers, and turn your heat off." He whipped his shirt over his head. "This is damp, but I'll roll it so I can create a barrier between us for 'porting. We're gonna need something."

I lifted my arm. My skin looked as lily white as it usually did, only as he touched his shirt to my skin, steam hissed from it.

"Ouch." He dropped his shirt. "How did Moyer not notice this heat? He touched you right before you burnt me."

"Maybe it started after he left?" Or maybe… "I can't harm the one I'm mated to. It's impossible because everything inside me would rally against it. Perhaps I controlled the temp with him?"

"Or he could be immune. As your mate, he physically holds the other half of your soul. A piece of you exists within him."

I gripped the ring swinging from my neck. "We need to check those records and find out if that's why. Go without me and find out what I need. I'll wait here."

"Leaving you alone isn't an option. Anyone could walk down this beach. No. It'll be easier to get Moyer to come back and simply have him test you as I did."

"He's busy—" My head swam, and dizzy, I dropped to my knees. "Whoa."

"What's wrong?" He crept closer then grumbled and backed away.

"My head." It throbbed, and as I focused within, a channel slowly formed and tapered outward. "Telepathy, I think."

"We've gotta get you out of here. Call to him."

"No." Only my mind splintered with a piercing intensity. My own voice echoed Guy's name over and over inside my head. Oh hell, I couldn't stop calling to him. "*Guy. Guy. Guy.*" His name spun out along the pathway I'd opened. "*Guy, please. Where are you? I need you.*" I slammed my hands on the ground and a vapor rose from under them. Oh no.

"*Silvie? Is that you?*" His voice was frantic, yet vividly clear in my mind.

"I can hear you. You have to come. Skill." The glassy granules within the sand fused together and hardened. *"Like right now. You have to come and get me out of here."*

"You're a telepath? You have a skill?"

"Fire skill."

"Hold on. The beach still?"

"Yes, and be careful. Apparently I'm hot. I just burnt Zayn."

"I'm coming."

A rush of wind hit me, and I pushed myself up. He stormed toward me and I shoved out a hand. "No. Stop. I might burn—"

He yanked me off my feet and into a smothering hold. "You don't feel hot to me."

"Guy." Why had he done that? "Didn't you hear me say I burnt Zayn?"

"Yeah." Pulling back a little, he eyed the protector. "He shouldn't have touched you. His fault."

"You don't feel her heat?" Zayn circled us. "It's pulsing off her in waves."

"I've got nothing, although what are these?" He tapped his booted foot on the shards of glass I'd hardened.

"That came from me." I gripped his shirtfront. "The fire skill runs through my family line. It's been two-hundred years since it last surfaced, but we'll find any information I need in our history books. Zayn will 'path Belle and have her search the volumes. Can you take me to the castle? I have no other way of getting back."

"Of course I can. Whatever you need, I'll provide."

Zayn shuffled back. "Let's hurry. She's getting hotter by the second." To Guy he said, "Follow my 'porting airstream."

"Lead the way." Everything darkened as Guy moved us through space and time. We arrived in the library, its thick double oak doors shut to any who might pass by. Rich mahogany shelves overflowed with burgundy leather-bound books, row after row of Peacio's history lay before us. Exactly what I needed.

"Thank you for bringing me home."

"You might need to be moved again. I'll stay."

"Belle's on her way." Zayn tapped his head. He'd 'pathed her. "She's just down the—"

"Silvie." Belle swung the doors wide and flew in. "Zayn said"—gasping, she bent over, hands on her knees—"that you have the fire skill. Ran all the way here. I really wish I could 'port."

"Me too." I hurried toward her. "I need help."

"Hey, hot, hot." She scrambled back, sweat popping up along her brow.

"Sorry. This is all new to me."

Guy whisked me up and set me down further away. "Silvie can't feel the heat she generates, and neither can I."

"Who are you?" Belle shoved dark locks over her shoulder and eyed him. "And why is there such a protective emotion emanating from you?"

"You're an empath?"

"Yes, and a protector. Now answer the question."

"I'm her mate." He moved in front of me, his back a solid wall.

"That would be released mate." I gripped his arm and tried to move my territorial mate. Nope. He wouldn't budge. "Belle, Guy's one of the warriors from Hope's outback station. Since my heat doesn't affect him, he 'ported me home."

A loud creak at my feet.

Belle stumbled back. "Okay, we've got to get you off the floor. Your heat is twisting the boards."

"I'm on it." Guy swung me into his arms.

"If I do more than warp the boards, get me out of here." I clung to him.

Belle took a wide berth around us then motioned to Zayn. "Come help me. There're a lot of books back there."

The two hurried into the darkened recesses.

I stole another look at the floor. "I can't believe I did that."

"I can't believe you 'pathed me." He smiled and nuzzled my hair.

"What are you doing?" Butterflies abounded in my belly. "I mean, don't do that."

"Mmm, you smell like sunshine, and your hair, it's a living flame with these strands of gold ablaze within the red."

"It's too red."

"I like red."

"We're getting rather close."

"Close is dangerous." He pulled back and looked into my eyes. "Sorry, gotta kiss you. Now."

"Wha—" His mouth stole over mine and whatever thoughts I had scattered, except for one. I wanted this kiss as much as he did. This moment couldn't be denied, so I kissed him as deeply as he kissed me. Oh, so wicked. I stroked his silky black hair. "We should have done this sooner," I mumbled against his lips. "So good."

"Hell, yes." He deepened our kiss.

I was lost in the sweet taste of him. My heart soared and my soul called to his. More. He was my mate, and it wasn't a bond to be broken. Except, damn it, we had.

"We should stop," he growled as he pulled away.

"Absolutely. What were you thinking?" Unable to help myself, I traced his full lips with a finger.

"I wasn't." He sucked my finger into his mouth, and I near exploded as heat raced through my veins.

"Silvie!" Belle screeched from the depths of the library. "Do you mind? Your emotions build on your skill, and you're causing a heat wave. I'm about to drown in my own sweat over here."

"Sorry, Belle." I glared at Guy. "Sheesh, that was your fault."

He grinned.

"He's not feeling repentant!" Belle yelled. "Silvie, please think cold thoughts. Lots of them. Right now."

"Do I have to?" A shiver chased down my spine. Yuck. Cold thoughts would suck.

"Yes." Carrying a burgundy leather book, Belle scurried out of the row. Her long hair lay limp down her back and the front of her blue swing shirt was wet. She tapped the book. "It says here cold thoughts are your first tactical response to lowering your heat. Imagine a snowy day, or ice trickling down your back. Maybe even a whole tub of ice and soaking in it. Whatever it takes, think cold."

"Just try it, Silvie." Panting, Zayn trudged out, his cheeks blotchy and red. "You're sucking all the moisture right out of the air."

"Okay, a tub of ice." Not wanting to, but not having any choice, I forced the image of a tub into my mind. Clumps of ice floated inside, and I shoved one foot in. Argh. I shuddered in revolt.

"That's working." Belle swept a hand through the air. "The room's still hot, but there's less heat coming off you. Whatever you're thinking, go further with it."

"Yeah, you would say that." I poked my tongue at her, but kept going. In my mind, I lowered my other foot into the tub and stepped fully in. "Shivers, that's cold."

"Are you okay?" Guy tucked me closer against him. "You've got goose bumps all over your arms and legs."

"Belle's a cruel empath."

"At least I'm a cooler one." She thumped the book down on the large oak desk and trailed her finger along the thick parchment paper. "It says your mated one will be immune to your heat, but not if you heat something surrounding you. It also records your skill will be a little uncontrollable until your rising, although that's no surprise. Our skills usually are."

The library doors burst open. Silas stormed in, his chest heaving under his loose-sleeved white shirt. He pulled his sword from the scabbard at his side and planted his booted feet wide. "Zayn 'pathed me, sis. You're mated to a warrior?"

"Hey." I waved, albeit feebly. "As it happens, he's right here."

Davio, Peacio's prince, prowled into the room in his battle leathers. He drew his sword and lifted it toward Guy. "Moyer. Once again we meet."

Oh hell. This was all I needed.

Chapter 3

"It's not what you think." Great. Now I had to face off against my brother and cousin.

"It looks exactly like what we're thinking, Silvie." Silas raked a hand through his closely cropped red-gold hair. "Zayn warned us you had a problem and to come as quick as we could. That problem is extremely evident."

"Guy's not the problem, and I thought since you all knew each other, you'd be on slightly friendlier terms than this."

"We're not killing him. That's friendly." Davio tipped his chin up a notch, which made his brown hair wisped with golden strands brush his shoulders. His dark eyes drew into slits as he stared at Guy. Close to six foot four, he matched my brother in height.

"He's tight with Faith and Hope. You wanna upset them?" Mentioning their mates should help, and where was Faith? Didn't this moment constitute a forewarning?

"You don't have to defend me, Silvie." Guy set me on my feet behind him then raised his sword toward Silas. "We never finished our last battle. It appears you'd like to."

"No. No. No." I shoved in front of him, coming squarely between them all. "Nobody fights my mate, I mean, my released mate."

Silas scrutinized me. "Released?"

"Yes, so just put that weapon away. He's here helping me, and that's all."

Silas tilted his head toward Guy. "You put yours away first."

"If you're scared, sure." Guy slid his blade home, although his hand remained firm on the hilt. "Your turn."

Huffing, he sheathed his sword. "Why must you keep turning up everywhere?"

"Because you and Loveria accepted the bond with my princesses. This all comes back to you."

"If you've finished helping my sister, then feel free to leave."

"Your empath just informed us her skill will be a little uncontrollable until she moves through her rising. If my mate requires my aid, she has it."

"What skill?" Face flushing, Silas plucked his shirt from his skin. "Is it just me, or is it hot in here?"

Davio sniffed the air. "I can't smell smoke, but did someone start a fire?"

"No," Belle intervened as she scanned the volume. "Silvie has the fire skill, and like her Carver ancestors, she can generate heat with the barest of thoughts and with the slightest swing in her moods. If she gets truly worked up, she has the ability to start a fire. If her fury takes her, then it says here, we'd all better duck."

"The fire skill?" Silas's blue eyes widened. "Sis, it's been so long, and you're skilled? Why didn't you say?"

"It only just happened. Guy brought me here because he's immune to my heat, and I was stuck in plain sight. Belle and Zayn have searched the records and told me how to control my temp." To Belle, I said, "You had me thinking cold thoughts before and that brought it down, but what happens if I start an actual fire? How do I extinguish that?"

"Don't you recall the tales our grandparents told us?" Silas crossed the room and ruffled my hair.

"Stop that." I did not have time for his brotherly shenanigans. "I wouldn't have asked if I'd remembered, silly."

"They used to say, once the one with the skill starts a fire, the only way to halt the flames is in the normal manner, with water."

"Yeah, thanks, Mr. Brightspark. I get that part. I meant how do I start and stop the fire when it comes from me? Is my skill completely controlled by my thoughts or is there more to it? I hardly want to blow something up by accident, or someone." No, don't say it. "Maybe even you." Yep, I couldn't help myself.

"Hmm, blowing someone up?" Guy's lips lifted. "It's a shame I'm the only one who's immune."

"Hey, only I'm allowed to tease my brother." I poked him in the chest, his rock hard chest. He must train daily to get those muscles. "Anyway, I've got a handle on my temp right now." But I wouldn't for long, if he stuck around. "You can go if you like."

"Ahh," Silas murmured as he rubbed his hands together. "Good job, sis. Dropping this one right out of the gate was a sure winner."

"Lucky you." Davio clapped Silas on the back. "That's one huge problem averted."

Guy scrubbed a hand over his face. "I still have to stick around to be sure. You know how the bond works."

"She's amongst family." Silas crossed his arms. "We'll watch over her, and you should ignore the bond. You did release each other."

"I think Guy should stay." Belle propped her butt on the desk. "He's offered, and it won't be for long. What we need to do is focus on Silvie's problem, on how she starts and stops the fire. I haven't read the answer yet."

"It'll be there." Faith swept into the room and hooked one thumb into the loop of her low-rise jeans. She slanted her head toward Davio. "Hello, honey." Well, about time she got here.

"You should be at school." Davio held out a hand to her.

"Silvie will need some serious help soon. I had forewarning." She crossed to him then leaned in for a kiss.

"Hey, everyone." Hope hopped into the room, yanking on one boot as she clutched the other under her arm. "Faith told me to hightail it here. Maslin dropped me off."

Her tan Stetson wobbled and Silas nabbed it and set it back on her head. "Maslin was here?" His gaze darkened.

"Don't go fixating on Maslin again. You promised."

"Your hair's wet." He steadied her as she tugged on her other boot. "You went swimming without me?"

"Yep." Done with her boots, she cupped his face. "Mmm, kiss. I need one now."

Okay, I understood how close Faith was with Davio, and Hope with Silas, but really? I was in crisis. I tapped the ground to get their attention. It didn't work. "Ah, excuse me, guys. Some serious help, remember?"

Faith grinned as she pulled back from Davio. "Oops, she's right. We'll pick this up later." She crossed to me. "I asked Hope to come since she can use her water skill to counteract your new ability with fire." She glanced at Guy. "Thank you for looking after her when it first came in."

"Yes, thanks from me too, Guy." Hope hugged him, then me. "Congrats on your new skill. It's amazing."

"Thanks. I didn't know all this would happen." She shouldn't have hugged Guy. I gripped his hand. Mine.

Faith winked at me. "I always wondered if a secondary reason existed for your fiery temper. You'll have to take care not to consume and devour. Your skill's about to heat up, and when it does, keep a level head." She struck a look at Silas and Zayn. "It'd be best if you two found some water. We need it, pronto."

"Gotcha." Silas flashed away and Zayn followed in his 'porting airstream.

Davio turned Faith by the shoulders. "What do you need me to do?"

"Make sure the windows are shut. We don't need a breeze stirring the flames."

"Flames?" Hmm, I really liked the sound of flames.

She rubbed my arms. "Don't get too excited. I need you to remain calm." She faced Belle. "Could you grab as many of the books from the shelves closest to Silvie and stack them behind the desk. We're after minimal damage."

"I'll help with that." Hope chased after Belle.

"Minimal damage sounds good." No damage at all sounded even better.

"Guy." Faith squeezed his shoulder. "Don't move from her side. You'll have to make certain she listens to you when things go beyond her control. The rest of us don't want to become toast."

"Toast?" Okay, I didn't like the sound of that either.

"I'll count you down, Silvie." Faith gave me a thumbs-up as she backed away.

"I'm going live now?"

"Three."

"Three already?" Could she not have given me more time? "What happened to counting down from ten? Everyone counts down from ten."

"Not me. Two."

Heat infused my blood and simmered out. "You could have given me—"

"One," she yelled as she dove behind the desk. The other girls lunged in behind her.

"Your hands!" Davio bellowed as he covered the girls and kept them down.

Tiny red and orange flames danced on my fingertips. Wow. This was one hot skill. "Am I emitting heat again?"

"A blast of it," Faith called out.

The air swirled and Silas and Zayn flashed in. Between them they carried a metal tub. As they lowered it to the floor, water sloshed over the sides. Zayn ducked behind it. "Looks like we got here just in time. You okay, Silvie?"

"I'm not sure." I curled my fingers inward and the fire played over my skin. It didn't burn, but soothed and stoked my need for more. Oh, I liked. "Actually, yes."

"Hope, you there?" Silas crawled toward the desk where he must have guessed she hid. "I've got your water."

"I'll come to you." She squirmed free of Davio. Silas met her halfway and covered her as they crawled back to the tub.

"Get that water into the air, Hope." Faith poked her head out.

"Onto it." Hope flicked her fingers, and the water lifted. The tubful rose in a gurgling bubble. She wiped the sweat from her brow. "Gee, I'd rather douse myself in this, but I've got you covered, Silvie."

"I don't want to be covered." The flames from my fingers dazzled in their brilliance. Ah, so nice, and with a single thought for more, the fire I'd brought to life spurted and lengthened.

"Cold thoughts!" Belle screamed. She was such a party-pooper.

"Right." Icy water. Ew. No, I couldn't do that, but a scorching hot day, where sunshine baked the ground, and me. Yes, now that I could do. Oooh, all that delicious warmth would be wonderful. So good.

"Silvie!"

I jerked as Guy snapped my name.

"Look." He pointed upward.

From my raised fingertips, the flames shot and skimmed the ceiling. "Holy moly. I can't believe I'm doing this."

"Not for long." Hope hit me with the water, square in the face. I knocked into Guy.

He righted me. "Hope, a little warning, please."

"I'll give her warning," I spluttered as I shook the water off and relit my fingers.

"No." Silas shoved in front of Hope. "Focus on your skill, Silvie, not the others here to aid you."

"I just want to singe her a little." I fed my thoughts with my rising anger, and the flames blazed brighter.

"You'll hate yourself if you do." Guy gripped my wrists and lifted my arms high. My fire licked the ceiling then chased across to the windows draped with red velvet. Oh, I so wanted to see that alight.

"Pull your fire back, Silvie." The shout came from Faith.

"I've got this." Hope pooled water from the ground and it gurgled and rose.

"No, Hope. This skill has lain dormant for far too long. It's time to give it free reign." Eyes closed, I envisaged a raging fire, a heat unlike any I'd ever known before, and it was all mine.

"Stop!" Davio blared, only I no longer cared.

"Listen to me, if no one else." Guy's black hair streamed behind him from the pulsing waves of my heat. "Find the control you need. Your skill can't rule you. That's not who you are."

"How would you know who I am? You decided not to stick around long enough to find out." The floorboards under me buckled and bent. "I want to burn."

"Look at me. I'll enchant you." The silver in his eyes swirled to life. "Heat has come and heat must go. Restore all to order, and make this one I hold whole." He locked our fingers tight together. "I'm here now. Don't let go of me."

He really wasn't going to leave me? My soul cried out for him. "I won't." I fought for control. Cold thoughts. Think only cold thoughts. My blood settled, aided by his spell. Order descended, incredibly fast. "Did I do it?"

"You did." Grinning, he smoothed his thumbs inside my palms. "Your fire is out."

It was, except the ceiling was scorched beyond repair.

"Look at the mess I've made."

"Get the curtains, Hope. They're smoking." Davio raced toward them.

"Got it." Hope sent a wash of water at them.

Zayn ran to help Davio, and the two hauled the soiled mess down.

"Hey." Faith twirled me around. "You did it. I can't believe what I just saw."

"I've destroyed the library." The damage I'd caused was intense.

Belle stared at the disaster. "You just need to learn some control. That's all."

"We'll watch over you until that day. Don't worry about the library. It can be repaired," Silas called from where he aided the others.

Together the men bundled the curtains up. Sooty water pooled at their feet, and Hope flicked her fingers and drew the water into the tub.

"How do I gain control?" This disaster couldn't happen again. Scorched ceilings and warped floor boards. Nah-uh.

"In the same way we all do." Guy cupped my cheeks. "Mind over matter, and don't worry about the mess. I can fix what you've damaged."

"You can? You'd do that for me? How?"

"With a spell." Hands directed upward, he chanted, "Above and below, repair and renew. All must be fused together, both the old and the new." Two streams of white light zoomed from his hands and arced toward the ceiling. One shimmered across its surface and the other rebounded and hit the floor. "Everyone, close your eyes. The light gains in brightness until it repairs all it needs to."

The dazzling light danced across both areas.

"You too, my mate." He covered my eyes as a wave of heat bathed us.

"Oooh, nice." I tried to pry his fingers away.

"A little bit longer."

I peeked through a gap. The good wood fibers knitted together, and the old disappeared. Soot fluttered down. "That's amazing."

"You weren't supposed to look." The floor boards creaked and rolled. Blackened dust plumed. Guy moved us back.

"I can handle the bright light. Thank you for this." On my tiptoes, I kissed his cheek.

"I'll collect the water I drenched you in. Hold still, you two." Hope swept her hands down Guy and me, drawing every last drop away. She floated the water back to the tub.

Davio heaved the roll of velvet onto his shoulder. "Good job, Moyer." He beckoned Faith to him. "Has she calmed for now?"

"Yes." She grabbed the trailing end and helped him. "Silvie, don't forget your skill is directly related to your emotions. If your excitement grows or your temper flares, it'll trigger your fire. 'Path me if you need me. I'll help Davio with this then head to school, but I can come in an instant. You only have to 'path me." She and Davio flashed away.

"She's right about the emotions." Belle patted her clammy cheeks. "I'm wiped out. I need a breather after this intense dousing of feelings. If you need me, 'path me too." She staggered out the door.

Poor Belle.

Silas gripped one end of the tub. "Moyer, if you don't mind, keep an eye on my sister until I get back. I can see you can handle her heat as the rest of us can't." He held out a hand to Hope. "I'll take you home."

She wrapped her arms around his waist since she couldn't 'port. Zayn grasped the other end of the tub, and the three of them shimmered and disappeared.

"I can't believe my brother actually left me alone with

you." What a surprise.

"I'm driven to see to your welfare. He knows that."

"Well, welfare aside, thank you. For a released mate, you've gone way beyond your duty. I think I'll take a breather like Belle did." I headed for the door. "Cooking always helps."

Guy followed, his gaze passing over the passageway's walls of textured silvery-white. The ceiling here was twice his height and held silver filaments inlaid into the corner plaster scrolling. "What are we cooking?"

"Lunch." My heart did a little happy dance he was here, but I should give him an out. "You don't have to stay."

"It's expected, and I want to."

"You do? Because expectation aside, I'd understand."

He snagged my hand as he caught up. "I'm staying."

Grinning, I tugged him around the corner and into my cozy kitchen. I lifted my arms with a flourish. "What do you think?"

"It looks totally out of place."

"I know, but I happen to like the conveniences of Earth." In the top red drawer, I found a white chef's apron. After slinging it over his head, I tied it off at the back. My happy place was back to being my happy place.

"Why am I wearing this?"

"It'll do since I don't have a jacket to give you."

"Why would I need a jacket?"

"To cover your chest." At least this apron kind of hid some of his impressive chest.

"That's what my shirt is for." His confused frown was so cute.

"It doesn't do a good enough job. You also look sharp in this apron. I wish I still had the chef's hat. Silas bought it for me as a gag gift, but I still love it."

"I'm not wearing a hat."

"Spoilsport." I skipped to the fridge. "This kitchen is almost identical to the one I had on Earth. I used to live close to Faith, but since she found out about Magio and her parentage, Carlisio sold the place. Do you have a modern kitchen at the station?" Our people didn't harbor technology as those on Earth did. We had no high-rises or cities of concrete here. No smoggy pollution either, which was probably why we lived easily to one-hundred and twenty.

"In the homestead, yes, but I'm only there half the time. The warriors' lodgings in Dralion though are well-equipped, what with travel being open to us." Guy wandered around my kitchen, skirting his finger along the edge of the bright red countertop as he made his way to the window. He scanned the area outside. "I can't believe I'm here. Peacio's fortress."

"You see anything out there that worries you?" I turned on the tap and washed my hands. "Apart from the garden? You've gotta watch those herbs. They'll attack at a moment's notice, shooting mint and chives everywhere."

"Cheeky." He swatted my bottom. "I'm simply making certain I can't be seen."

"No one would harm you if you're with me." I nudged him to wash his hands.

"Well, there's a bonus to having a mate reside in the enemy's home." He scrubbed his hands. "What are we making for lunch?"

"Fresh jelly donuts with jam and cream. I feel like something sweet."

"Mmm, my mother used to make fresh bread each morning. I love the aroma which infuses the air. It's always been a favorite of mine."

"I wish I could have met your mother." I pulled out what I needed from the pantry and fridge. "It's been ages since someone cooked with me. Everyone's always so busy these days. We'll make two batches, one of long donuts, and the other round. Faith and Hope like the ringed ones with the colored icing." I dug out two bowls and passed one to Guy. "You're in charge of the girls' favorite."

"No problem." He plunked his bowl on the counter. "Show me what to do."

From the overhead shelf, I snagged the recipe book then flicked it to the correct page. "It's all very easy. The key with making fresh bread is not to forget the yeast, to knead well and to allow the dough to rise."

"I can't believe I'm making donuts. In Loveria Castle. Donaldo would throw me in the dungeons if he saw this."

"Then it's just as well your king can't see you." I scooped flour into a sieve and held it over his bowl. "Here. Take over and get shaking."

"Get slaying would be better." His side sword was hidden under his apron, but still within easy reach.

"There will be no blood shed in my kitchen."

"No, there's donut making instead."

I added a pinch of salt as he sifted, and then tapped the recipe. "Keep your eyes on the prize. I want to see some magic performed. You're an enchanter after all."

"Yes, my hot-headed one." He got busy. A plume of flour rose and wafted onto his midnight hair. He added the rest of the ingredients and mixed.

I prepared the donut dough. The long ones with jelly were Silas and Davio's favorite. When younger, they'd eaten them only after blowing the dusted icing sugar from the top into each other's faces. So funny.

"Who cooks for you in Dralion?" I kneaded, and he followed suit with his dough.

"The cooks. There's a communal dining hall where the warriors eat."

"What about at the station?"

"Again, food is prepared for us. There's a chef at the homestead." He rolled his dough into a ball and set it carefully into his bowl. "Do I drape a towel over this? I remember my mother used to do that."

"Yes, and sit it in the sunshine." I swiped two clean towels from the drawer and tossed him one.

"This has brought back some nice memories." He laid it over the rim with quiet reverence. "Thank you."

"Any—ah, sorry." What was I thinking? He couldn't come back anytime. I scurried to the sink and rinsed my hands.

"It's all right. I understand." Arms around me, he pressed his broad chest to my back and thrust his hands under the water with mine. "What's a normal day like for you?"

"School, homework, hanging out in my kitchen. If I'm lucky, a good dose of bickering with Silas and Davio thrown in. What about you?"

His breath fanned my cheek. "I train in the mornings with the sword, and then aid Hope as she needs at the station. In the afternoons, I study my craft. Each spell requires rigorous testing."

I grabbed a cloth, patted my hands dry then his. "And in the evenings?"

"Whatever's waiting for me in Dralion. Donaldo understands, without my father to aid me, I'm studying my skill alone. I'm allowed certain leeway."

I faced him. "You make Wincrest sound almost human."

"He is."

"No, he's not." I straightened his collar tangled by the apron string. "He's a tyrant."

He dipped his head, touched his nose to mine. "I've told you my allegiance is to my king and country. You won't sway me otherwise."

"I wasn't trying to." I would never do that. I had no right to. Eyes closed, I fought back the strong emotions taking me. "I wish things were different."

"So do I." His voice was whisper soft. "Gotta kiss you again. Sorry."

His lips descended on mine. Oh boy. Hot, and so yummy. He deepened the kiss and a delicious heat stole through my veins. Arms around his neck, I sank into him. He was all muscle, and lots of it, a tower of strength in more ways than one.

"Okay, that's good," he mumbled against my lips. "No, maybe a little bit more." He devoured, and I didn't stop him. I held on tight for the ride of my life. Sooo good.

"Uh-hum. Fire."

Faith rapped the countertop, blond hair whooshing about her shoulders.

"Can't I leave you alone for one minute? There's fire sizzling from your fingertips, Silvie."

"What?" I blew on the tips, but that only made the flames lick higher.

"Don't feed them. Think cold. And why are you kissing Guy? I got forewarning and had to hurry this time. If you get hot and heavy with him then watch your temp, otherwise you'll burn down your kitchen."

"The kissing's my fault." Guy yanked the fridge open and planted me in front of it. His lips lifted in a slow smile. "I couldn't help myself."

Cool air washed over me. The flames spluttered and died. "Okay, so kissing isn't good."

Still smiling, Guy inspected the tips then ran his thumbs over them. "Not good at all."

A new surge of heat thrummed through me at his close touch. "You wanna do it again?"

He backed away. "Don't test me."

"Ah, excuse me." Faith leaned against the countertop and eyed Guy. So, you two"—she flicked a hand between us—"have changed your minds?"

"No." Guy cleared his throat. "What you saw is not what it looked like."

"I didn't see any kissing?"

"I'm only here to aid Silvie, as you asked."

"Aiding Silvie requires talking, not kissing." She lifted the towel from one of the bowls. "Hmm, donuts. Silvie never lets me cook with her."

"Yeah, because you burn everything, and it's just donuts. I don't see what the problem is."

"Well, this dough has risen, and I'd say because of the extreme heat in here."

"Great." I slid the bowl across and scooped it out. "See, kissing has its benefits."

"I'm sure it does." She smirked then straightened her lips. "You want me to turn the oven on?"

"Yep, and grab me a tray while you're there." I rolled my dough into a long sausage shape. Guy cut and shaped his into circles. "You're a quick learner."

"I have a good teacher, but since we're here, we should speak about how I'm supposed to assist you, and not in the kitchen."

"Don't ask me. Try Miss I-see-the-future." I set each of my donuts on the tray.

Faith nibbled her lower lip. "Um, I only know the forewarning's gone again now you two are talking. At least we're back on the right track."

"But what track is that?" Guy set his donuts beside mine then carried the tray to the oven and slid it inside. "It's not like Silvie can get to Dralion, so whatever she comes up with has to take effect here."

"I don't like that Silvie's even involved."

"Neither do I." He shoved the oven door shut. "This is Dralion's business, not hers."

I cleared the countertop as they continued to mutter between themselves. What Guy didn't understand was, the girls were my business. Faith was a sister to me, and Hope was mated to my brother. I couldn't get closer to the girls if I tried.

"Guy." I faced him, my temper on the rise. "With Wincrest effectively trying to marry the girls off, it's as if I've been set the mission of halting the escalation of our war. I don't think I'd mind meeting him at all, if that's the case." No, not now I had the fire skill. Oh, the things I could—

"Fire." Jumping, Faith pointed at my hands. "Quick, extinguish it."

Chapter 4

"I've got this." Guy slung a towel around my hands and snuffed the fire. "Silvie, you're never meeting Donaldo. Now, watch your emotions. You can't keep lighting up like this."

"I don't see I have a choice." I flung the towel away. "And stop telling me what to do."

"Put these on." Faith tossed me my oven mittens and I shoved them on. "You only come up with the answer to my problem. You don't get to expand on it, and I've certainly not set you the mission of halting the war."

"I didn't say halt the war, but the escalation of it, and yes, you kinda have."

"No. I. Haven't."

"Stop arguing with me, or my temper's really gonna explode. And at this rate, I bet neither of you will even listen to me when I do come up with something."

"We'll listen, but we'll action it. Not you." Faith plucked her violet t-shirt from her skin. "You still haven't calmed down. It's getting hotter in here."

"It's my kitchen. You're welcome to leave it if you want."

"When you've made donuts. Ha, I don't think so." She peered through the oven's glass door. "They're almost ready. Come and check."

I stomped across, wishing she would get the point and

leave. Only sure enough, the donuts had turned a delicious golden brown. Their heavenly scent wafted into the air as I opened the oven door. Faith all but drooled over them.

"Nose out."

"Why don't you ever say nose in?"

"Because you do that automatically." I tipped the donuts onto a wire rack, and she lifted her nose into the air and let out the loudest sigh. "Mmm. You're forgiven."

"For what?"

"Arguing with me." She pinched one of the donuts, fumbled then lost her grip. "Ouch, hot."

"Of course they're hot. Go and whip the cream, and if you do a good job, I'll forgive you for arguing right back."

"That's the worst thing about cooking. You have to wait before you can eat." She yanked open the drawer and pulled out a beater.

"My mother used to cut a few slices from the end of the loaf to cool it quicker." Guy slid a knife free of the wooden knife block. Using it, he cut a perfect slit for the jam and cream down the center of each of the long donuts. "But in this case, this should do."

"Excellent." Faith's stomach rumbled from across the room. "Now that smells even better."

"Okay, I can tell my sister's cooked." Hand-in-hand with Hope, Silas strode in through the swing door. His red-gold hair was wet, as was Hope's. They must have been for a swim. "I swear I smelt donuts all the way from the watering hole. Was I right, sis?"

"You have a big nose."

"No, I actually have an acute sense of smell." He grinned as mischievously as he had when we were kids. "You want me to set the table?"

"Yes, where's Davio?"

"Right here." He stepped into the room in his chunky

leather boots and made a beeline for Faith. "You snuck away from school early, love."

"Silvie got a little too hot to handle again. I had to skip the last class to come and cool her down." She pulled the beater from the cream and licked the end. "She's in a very tempestuous mood today. Try and steer clear of her."

"Sounds like someone else I know." He dipped one finger into the bowl.

"I'm not tempestuous." She smacked his hand. "That's my cream."

"You're not? Are you sure?" He kissed the corner of her lips where a smear of cream remained. Or not, as now was the case.

"Hey, that was mine too." She shoved him back. "Go whip your own cream."

"Merge your mind with mine." He caught her between him and the counter. "I need the contact."

"I'll merge when I feel like it. Stop trying to get your way."

He laughed then kissed her, putting a complete stop to her arguing. Yeah, she had to have finally merged since she let out a long, appreciate sigh. She and Hope both had the skill, and it connected them to their mates in a very personal way.

"Right, that's enough, you two." Silas knocked Davio's shoulder as he headed to the crockery cupboard. "I'm hungry, and those donuts smell too good not to eat."

"I'll help you." Hope held out her hands and he passed her the lunch plates.

The glasses in hand, Silas led the way out to the dining room. Davio and Faith followed with the cutlery.

"Is your kitchen always this busy?" Guy caught his mother's ring dangling at my neck and stroked it.

"Pretty much. I like having you here in it." Really liked it. Smiling, I passed him another bowl. "You get to prepare the smooth yellow icing."

He passed the bowl back, rested against my back and snuggled. "I've missed this feeling of home."

"You don't want to make the icing?"

"I want to watch you make it." Nuzzling my neck, he purred.

With his rumble heating my skin and tingling my toes, I got to work on the icing. "How difficult is it without your father?"

"Two years has been far too long." He reached past me and stole the first donut I'd iced. He smacked his lips together then murmured, "Ahh, good. Real good."

"Try a long donut." I squirted in the cream and added a dollop of jam and passed it across.

"Even better," he mumbled around a mouthful.

I cupped his jaw. "The silver in your eyes is lighting up."

"At least your hands aren't."

"No, I seem to have gained some control over my emotions, even while you're this close. Hopefully it'll hold. Faith will soon let me know if it doesn't." I ruffled his black hair, removing the dusting of flour still on the ends.

"I'm glad she's here to watch over you."

"We look out for each other. We always have."

He eyed the door the others had left by. "Since you've got plenty of aid on hand, and you appear stable, I should go."

"Can't you stay a little longer? Please?" I didn't want him to go, not even into the next room.

"Loveria and Carver are here. They seem okay with me still hanging around, but I doubt it'll last long." He undid the ties of his apron and pulled it over his head. "Thank you for loaning me this."

"I want you to stay." I couldn't stop my needy request. "I mean, don't feel you have to rush off." Yeah, that wasn't going to cut it either.

"I'd like to stay, which is another reason why I should go." He pressed the apron into my hands.

"You're worried about our bond building?"

"Aren't you?"

"I should be." I just couldn't consider that when he was this close, though.

"We have to take care, Silvie. Any time we spend together should be kept to a minimum."

"Ooo-kay." I could hardly argue that fact. "It was nice having you here."

"It was nice learning how to make the most delicious donuts ever." He fingered a lock of my hair then lowered his hand to his side. "It's hard not to touch you."

"Same." I wanted to touch him, so badly.

"Tomorrow evening, my mate." He bent his head in a short bow

So proper, and so fast, he flashed away.

Gone.

My mated one had left me again.

I swirled a hand through the air where he'd been, my heart as heavy as a stone. This moment hurt. Not good.

"Is lunch ready yet?" Faith bounced into the room. "The masses are hungry."

"They're all done. I've got dinner to prepare for Zayn's family next." I slid the dish to her, my appetite gone. "Take these in for me, okay?"

"Sure." She nudged my shoulder with hers. "So Guy left?"

"Yeah." I slumped onto the countertop and stroked his mother's ring. "I think I'm in trouble."

"What did you do?"

"I have feelings for him."

"You don't like having them?"

"What do you think? He's the last enchanter in his line and Wincrest expects him to marry another warrior woman. We've released each other, and there's no going back."

She rubbed my back. "That sucks."

"Big time." I dropped my chin into my upturned palms, wishing things could be different. They never would be. "Did you know he lost his mother when he was young? This is her ring."

"He gave you his mother's ring? No way."

"It was her last wish, that he pass it along to his mated one." I eased myself upward. "Don't tell anyone else, okay? It's kind of private."

"You got it." She gave me a hug, squeezing me tight. "Will you be all right?"

"Yeah. I can deal. What with your problem, my fire skill and Guy coming and going, at least I'm not twiddling my fingers."

"Well, you've always got me, and that'll never change. I can probably promise a ton of future problems for you to fix too." Violet eyes twinkling, she picked up the dish. "I'll go feed the hounds before they chase me in here."

"Thanks. I'd like some quiet time, just me and my kitchen."

"You got it."

Definitely no finger twiddling. I got busy with the night's upcoming meal, preparing a deep lasagna dish that would feed an army, or certainly Zayn's family of twelve. Afterward, I made a gooey chocolate brownie, one large enough for double servings. Without a doubt, there was plenty for all.

As the skies darkened out the window, I cleaned up.

Yeah, it was time to change, and to take this mountain of food to where it was needed.

I hurried down the passageway to the north terrace and raced up the gray marble staircase to my rooms on the second floor.

I crossed my sitting area, a space which was all mine, and one I adored. Gold throw pillows graced two long comfy couches in deep red. Those two colors had always bathed me in their warmth. No wonder, really, that I loved the colors of a blazing fire now I'd received the fire skill. I skimmed my fingers over some of my favorite cook books stacked on a redwood bookshelf behind my study-desk. Yellow notes poked from between many of the well-worn pages, beckoning me. So many recipes I had to get to. After finals there'd be more time.

I continued on to my dressing room. From my drawers, I grabbed a pair of skinny red jeans and a soft yellow blouse embroidered with red on the capped sleeves. Nice bright colors to keep bumping up my mood. Cooking for Zayn's family had helped. I just had to keep busy. I dressed then searched the bathroom vanity for my wide-tooth comb. My reflection in the mirror over the basin showed a fright, although nothing unusual for me after hours in a hot kitchen. My hair was a frizzy bird's nest, the strands of red-gold matted together. I gently detangled the knots then set a clip at each side, gold with a small ruby stone, the set gifted to me from Silas for our last birthday. Okay, that was a little better. With a touch of berry flavored lippy, I was done.

Hmm, what would Guy be doing now? He'd said in the evenings he attended to whatever awaited him in Dralion. He'd likely be seeing to Wincrest's bidding then. Being mated to a warrior really wouldn't have worked, or at least that's what I'd keep telling myself.

What I needed to do was get some control over my fire skill, sort the girls' problem, and then I'd no longer need Guy. Not even the smallest bit.

Today had definitely seen my reliance on him grow, when I shouldn't need him at all. I was an independent woman.

"Silvie, it's Zayn. You ready?"

I tapped my head and smiled. Nice. I liked the telepathic skill. *"Hey."* I scurried from my room. *"Everything's made. I'm coming down now. I'll be five minutes."*

"Great. How's your afternoon been? Any more fire?"

"Just a touch, but Faith warned me, so I didn't burn

anything. Sorry about not getting to show you around. What'd you get up to without me?"

"I took another swim at your beach. Oh, I see the chocolate brownie. You'd better hurry or I might start on it."

"Don't you dare." I picked up my pace, fairly flying down the passageway. Whoa. Too fast. Not like me at all. I almost took out the vase of white roses perched on the recessed wall shelf as I skidded around the doorway into my kitchen. Bending over, I grabbed in a breath. "Phew, I'm here. Fingers out."

Grinning, he licked his thumb. "Too late, and I thought you said five minutes."

"My speed's up." I grabbed the brownie. "Look at that hole. I'll tell your mother you did that."

"Yeah, she won't be surprised." Still grinning. "Hey, you want to work on your fire skill tomorrow? I'll be done with my day's duties by the time you finish school, and I found this amazing spot about twenty miles farther down the beach from where we were today. It's secluded and perfect for what you'll need."

"Sounds great." He was the best, for wanting to help me.

He tucked the shirttails of his loose-sleeved white shirt into his brown rawhide pants. He must have dressed on the run. "I can't wait to see all you can do. You could whip some serious butt with your skill."

"You mean burn it." I nudged the lasagna dish toward him and kept the warm brownie in my hands. "Zip-zap, please."

"You got it." He scooped up the dish with one hand and held my arm with the other. "Be prepared for a lot of noise. That's the only warning I'll give you."

I laughed as we 'ported, and moments later we arrived on the stony road between the woodland ranges and the village of Merodyne. I adored the countryside, the remoteness and the quiet. Moonlight bathed the tree tops a silvery hue, and from a sprawling wooden-shingled home, smoke rose eerily then vanished on the wind.

"How gorgeous." Lanterns lit the square-cut front windows, sprinkling a yellow glow over the beamed porch railing. "I can just see you running about these woods as a kid."

"Yeah. But I'm not sure where all the noise I promised you is."

"Do you come home often?" He had rooms in the village closest to the castle where an arena, training facilities and a dining hall provided all our protectors needed.

"A couple of times a week, but only for a short—"

"Zayn!" A girl of about ten bounded out the front door and across the front yard dotted with yellow flowers. Her blond ponytails bobbed and her grin slashed from ear to ear. She plowed into him, puffing from her mad dash. "Oh my goodness, that smells yummy. Please say I'm allowed to eat that now. Is that cheese on the top?" Her nose was in the dish.

"Yes. Giggi, say hi to Silvie."

"Hi, Silvie. Mmm, what have you got? That smells like chocolate." She wafted across to me.

"It's a brownie, with loads of gooey chocolate for sure. It's nice to meet you, Giggi."

"Same. Can I take that for you?"

"Be careful, it's heavy." I passed it across.

She winked and rushed back to the house. "Last one inside misses out."

"Well, she's a delight." I'd always wished for a sister, but it was only Silas and me. Thankfully Faith had filled that void.

"Giggi's always on the go. Come and meet everyone else."

He led the way up the front step and through the opened door. The heat blasting into the entrance from the living room drew me toward the doorway. A fire blazed in the hearth. I'd never want to leave this room if I lived here. Two teens lazed on knitted throw cushions, and three younger ones sat cross-legged on colorful mats playing with thin painted sticks. Each took a turn, adding their stick to the growing platform. This was a game of skill, and one I'd loved playing with Silas as a child.

I leaned into Zayn. "I always won this game. Silas had such big hands and always knocked the sticks down."

"I had the same problem. I've won that game twice, ever, and that was purely by chance." Lifting his hand toward his siblings, he called out, "Hey, everyone, this is Silvie."

A chorus of "hellos" came at me, and I waved back.

"Come on. We'll take this dish through to the kitchen." I had to force myself to follow him down the hallway and away from the fireplace's heat, the only incentive being he'd said *kitchen*. "Here we are."

Oh, nice. Brass pots and pans hung over a wood-fired stove, and beside it, a cane basket overflowed with kindling. "Since your home has two fireplaces, I believe I might move in."

He chuckled. "I'm taking you to the next village bonfire night. You'll love that."

"Yes, please, if you can drag me out of this room." His mother's kitchen was clearly the hub of the home. On the scuffed wooden countertop, a pail overflowed with ripened red apples. Tasty. And beyond, a wide dining area held a chunky pine table draped with a crocheted cloth. Giggi knelt on one of the slatted bench seats before it and set the brownie on top.

"Where's Mum, Giggi?"

"I don't know, but I'll go find—"

"I'm right here." Zayn's mother swished into the room in brown skirts and an apron. Long golden hair, the same shade as Zayn's, swung in a thick braid down her back. His mother's eyes widened as she took in the dishes. "Oh, that looks delicious."

Giggi pointed to the corner of the brownie. "I didn't do that."

"I'm sure you didn't. Thanks, hon. You go and call your father in. He should be out by the woodshed. Let him know we have a guest." She smiled at Zayn. "Pop the lasagna on the table,

Mr. Taste-tester."

Zayn grinned and slid his dish where she'd said. "It's gets a ten out of ten, if you're wondering."

"I'm sure it does." She crossed the room and grasped my hands. "Lovely to meet you, Silvie. Thank you so much for bringing dinner. I can't believe this is the first time we've met, although I do remember seeing you in the arena stands at Zayn's rising. I'm Briarlee. Zayn speaks about you all the time."

"He does?" Zayn's cheeks had flushed.

"Mum, what did you do to your hands?"

"I picked berries today." She twiddled her stained fingers in the air. "I'll try and have another scrub at them." At the sink, she picked up a slab of soap, one close to a half pound of butter in size. "Tell me all about your day off, hon."

"Silvie took me to her favorite beach."

"You two went out together?" She peered over her shoulder at him. "That sounds intriguing."

"It's not what you think."

"How do you know what I'm thinking?" Her hands disappeared within the mound of bubbles she'd built.

"It's obvious. Anyway"—he scratched the back of his neck—"Silvie came into her fire skill today."

"What?" She flung her hands into the air and suds flew. A blob landed on Zayn's head. "The fire skill, but that's—wow. We haven't seen that skill in far too long."

"I didn't have very good control of it. First day and all." But I would.

"That'll only take a little training." She nabbed a towel and patted Zayn's head. "The fire comes from your fingertips, right?"

"Yep." I lifted my hands, and with barely a thought, the fire flickered to life.

Eyes wide, she reared back. "Oh, that's incredible."

I waved my hands in front of me and the glowing red and

orange sparks licked higher.

"Okay, that's also hot." She edged further away. "How do you put it out?"

"Thinking of cold stuff, or getting doused in water. I prefer neither." Still, I got down to the nasty business of conjuring the iciest winter day possible. A chill soon penetrated my bones, and I shivered and stamped my feet. Ick.

"That's very clever. Your flames are out."

"You controlled that quickly." Zayn examined my hands, turning them over. "It's obviously better for you to get a handle on things as soon as the fire appears. We'll practice whenever you wish. You'll need to be ready for your rising when it comes."

Oh boy. I didn't want to think about my rising, the time when our skills came to fruition and burned at three times the strength. I would need a mountain of control for that. "You're really up for helping me train?"

Briarlee patted my shoulder. "Of course he is. My son won't have a problem keeping an eye on you." She pinched Zayn's cheeks. "Ahh, my firstborn who has the battle skills. I'll never forget your rising."

I'd been there that day in the arena too, just a few months ago. A massive crowd had gathered and packed the spectator's seating, eager to see him become a fully-fledged protector. It was an honored occasion, when one relied on their closest to get them through the long hours ahead. Down on the sandy-floored arena, Zayn had worn his black combat leathers, headgear and guards. His power that day had been phenomenal.

One's rising was the most spectacular event to watch, and Zayn's just so as he'd drawn his sword against one opponent after another. Even Davio and Silas had taken turns, not long past their own risings, but neither had been able to keep up with him.

"I hope I manage mine as well as you did yours, Zayn."

"You will, and if you wish it, I'll be there."

"That will be a sight to see." Briarlee smiled. "As is your dinner. I'll go check on where Giggi got to. I can't let your food spoil." She hurried away.

"Your mother is lovely."

"She's also nosy, and probably won't stop quizzing me about you from now on." His blue eyes twinkled. "Have you thought about joining the protectors once your rising is done?"

"I have culinary school. It's not something I want to—oh, she's fast." The sound of stampeding feet was impossible to miss.

"Another warning." Zayn whisked me off my feet and tucked me into the corner behind him. "Beware of the tribe."

Chapter 5

"*Oh my goodness. I did not see that forewarning coming.*" Faith's voice rang clear in my head.

"*You see everything, so that's impossible. And I hardly call what you saw a forewarning. You were being nosy. You shouldn't spy on other people. It only means you'll see things you shouldn't.*" I yanked my yellow cotton sleep-shorts on and hauled my white singlet over my head as I readied for bed. "*I'm going to sleep. It's been a long day.*"

"*Zayn's becoming too attached to you. He had his hands on you during the family dinner.*"

"*Not in the way you're implying.*" She was totally overreacting. "*He's kind and considerate, plus I have to move on.*"

"*With Zayn?*"

"*We're friends, and I'm not supposed to be with Guy.*"

"*I get that. Hold on.*" She was gone one moment then back the next. "*Oops, the water beckoned to Hope and she just walked straight into the watering hole, boots and all.*"

"*You're in the outback?*"

"*Yeah, she was driven to have a moonlit swim. Crazy, anyway, you've got enough to do right now without adding any further complications, that being Zayn.*"

"*Zayn's offered to help me train.*"

"Then I'll ask Guy to help you too."

"What? No."

"Yes." She broke our connection.

Argh, unbelievable. I had to spend less time with Guy, not more.

I slid under my bedcovers and stared at the overhead lightshade. The crystal drops teetering from the edges of the delicate chandelier shimmered with gold from the light, like a small burst of sunshine.

"Silvie." Guy's deep voice rumbled inside my head.

"Let me guess. Faith just spoke to you?" She and I really needed to have words. That's if she'd ever listen to me.

"It's just as well she did." His words held a lethal undertone. *"Are you seeing Zayn?"*

"He's a protector. I need his aid."

"That's my job."

"Not since you're the one who said any time we spend together should be kept to the bare minimum."

"I can't talk about this across a distance. Give me a second."

"A second for what? Guy?"

"I'm here."

"Where?"

"Outside. Which window is yours? There're balconies everywhere."

"I'm about to go to sleep. Go back home."

"No. Tell me where you are before the guards catch me. I don't need to end up in the cells like my father has."

"I can't believe you're here. You're as bad as Faith at listening. Second floor. North terrace." I shoved back the golden covers and raced to the balcony doors. Holding the thick golden curtain to one side, I found the door handle and pushed it open.

He shimmered into view, his chest rising and falling with each deep breath. Then he strode toward me and pulled me into his arms. "Don't ever say that to me again."

"Say what?" I mumbled into his chest covered in soft blue cotton.

"That he's a protector and you need his aid."

Territorial mate was back. "Then you shouldn't have opened our link."

He kicked the door shut and walked me backward. "Nice room. It's all yours?"

"Yes, and what are you doing here? This is crazy."

"No. What's crazy is, I've gotta kiss you and it can't wait." His mouth descended onto mine, hot and heavy as he explored every inch like a man on a mission.

Oh boy. So good. No. So bad. Where was my focus?

He tumbled me onto the bed, and I pushed him back to get some space. An inch, but one valuable inch. "You need to go."

"After we talk."

"On my bed?"

"It's a nice bed." He arched one very cute eyebrow.

"It's late." Great. How was I to enforce some distance when he was like this?

"I was up working for Donaldo."

"So that makes it okay? Sure, why don't you just make yourself at home then?" I was aiming for sarcastic, but didn't quite pull it off. Part of me still longed to have him here.

"Thank you. I will." He unbuckled his sword belt and propped his blade against the headboard. "I realize I shouldn't have come."

"Totally." I shuffled to the top of the bed and stuck my feet under the covers.

"Let's sort the girls' dilemma. We'll make it a top priority." After toeing off his boots, he rolled into bed.

"All I know is, I have to figure out a way to stop an impending courtship. I have no idea how to go about it, Guy."

"Neither do I, but you're the key, and I can't aid you from a distance, no matter what I said." He eased his head onto my pillow and slid a hand around my waist. With a yank, he toppled me against him.

"Oomph. You're getting far too comfortable."

"Because I can't get one fiery redhead out of my mind." He nuzzled into my hair, inhaling slowly. "You smell delicious."

"Then stop smelling me. So, how are you going to aid me?" Oh boy, he smelt good too, of fresh air and sunshine, two things I could never get enough of.

"In whatever way you need." He stroked my back.

"That's not aiding." Although, his gentle caress relaxed me further, and I couldn't hold back a soft sigh.

"Then let's brainstorm."

"It's almost midnight. My brain is ready to shut down. It's certainly not thinking straight."

"Then we'll talk in the morning."

"I have school."

"What about after school?"

"I have training, and we've already agreed to meet tomorrow evening."

"We should meet sooner. You've gotta make some time for me."

"No, what I've gotta do is make some time for sleep." I rolled to my side, turning away. That's better. Instill some distance. "We'll chat tomorrow night. Now go home."

"I'll leave once you're asleep."

"You should leave now." I tried for a stern tone, but a yawn escaped me. Maybe it was best just to ignore him.

I drifted as the minutes ticked by, him so deliciously warm behind me. Then he wrapped his arms around me. Oh, blisss.

My soul-bound one held me, and if only for this small moment in time, I'd never forget. "Goodnight, Guy."

"Sweet dreams, my mate."

* * * *

I awoke to warm breath fluttering across my cheek and a man's arms banded tightly about me.

Oh my goodness. No way.

Clearing the sleep from my eyes with my knuckles, I stared at him. Guy still slept in my bed, his coal-black hair a rumpled mess and his chin sharp with a razz of stubble.

"Hey." I shook his shoulder.

"It's too early." He cupped the back of my head and tucked me back against him. "I'm not ready to wake up yet."

"You're still in my bed."

"I know. It was damn impossible to leave with you sleeping so sweetly." He dragged one eyelid open. "You feel tense."

"I've got school."

"So you said last night. What time is it?" He reached for my wrist and checked the digital display on my Earth watch. "Eight. I'll drop you off."

"Have you been to my high school before?"

"I've never had a reason to, but I'll follow Faith's 'porting airstream so I'll know the way."

"If Faith's going, I'll catch a ride with her."

"In case there's an emergency, like with your fire skill, I need to be able to get to you fast."

"That's what I have family and friends for. You're the only one I shouldn't be calling on." I wriggled down then crawled out the moment I had enough space. "Don't worry about me. I have everything sorted."

"Like training with Zayn?" He propped himself on his elbows, his expression grim. "You just had dinner with him."

"Yes, I did. Get over it." I snatched a pair of white cotton shorts and a cheery red tank top from my dresser.

"You turning to another man isn't right. I don't care for it."

"Of course you don't, but you've given up your place in my life. We're both moving on, remember?" I headed to the bathroom and closed the door with a loud bang, not waiting for his answer. All remained quiet on the other side. Deep in my heart, I wasn't ready to move on either, but I wouldn't tell him that. I hardly needed to lay my heart on the line for a man who didn't want me.

Shoving away from the door, I sighed. Those feelings were there, like I'd told Faith, and him staying the night had only made them deepen.

Still, nothing I could do about it. I pushed on, changed, brushed my teeth and combed my hair, still without a whisper of noise from beyond. Good, he must have gotten the point and gone.

I snuck to the door and opened it a crack. Yep, definitely gone. I strode out.

"Those shorts are too short."

My heart almost lurched from my chest. He was here. I spun around. And why did he have to look so hot? He'd changed, and his blue jeans clung to his hips. "What are you doing back?"

He sauntered across, midnight-blue cuffs rolled to his elbows. "Making sure you don't go out like that." He pressed me against the wall. "Plus, we still need to talk about Zayn. He's not training you."

"Yes. He. Is. And I like these shorts."

He slid his hands over my hips and along the frayed edge of my shorts. "No. He. Isn't."

I tried to pry his fingers loose, only his grip remained firm.

"*Silvie.*" Zayn's voice bounced inside my head. "*I'm trying my hand at bacon and eggs. I wanted to cook you breakfast as a thank you for last night.*"

"*You're in my kitchen?*"

"*Yep. Nothing's burnt yet, but that could change at any minute. Cooking's not really my forte.*"

"*I'm coming, only Guy's here and insisting on taking me to school. We'll give him anything that's charred.*"

"Who are you speaking to?" Guy's gaze narrowed to slits.

"Zayn. He made breakfast."

The muscle in his jaw ticked. "In your kitchen? For you?"

"Yes, and be nice."

"Ha, right." Everything darkened as he 'ported us.

We arrived, and I prepared myself for the battle to come.

Zayn flipped bacon onto a dish next to a mound of scrambled eggs. He appeared ready for arena training with his sword and daggers sheathed in place. "Well, if it isn't the warrior who enjoys spending a little too much time on Peacian soil."

"You look ready to battle." Guy pumped out his chest. "You want to train with a real opponent for a change?"

"Do you know one?" Zayn stroked the hilt of his sword, a sly smile lifting his lips.

Grrreat. A warrior and a protector facing off in my kitchen. I stepped between them and grabbed the dish. "Okay, this is ready." I pressed it into Guy's hand and urged him ahead of me into the dining room. Cutlery sparkled on the tabletop next to glasses of orange juice and a central plate of buttered toast. Zayn had gone to a lot of trouble.

"Ladies first." Zayn pulled out a chair for me.

"Ah, thanks. It was so nice of you to cook."

Guy let out a low growl, thrust out the chair beside mine and plunked himself down. "*Has he cooked for you before?*" He snapped the words along our link.

"*No.*" I served the bacon and eggs, giving the men the largest portions. Hopefully that would keep their mouths busy.

Guy snatched his fork and dug in. "*Do you two eat together regularly?*"

"*Sometimes.*" I munched on my eggs.

"*I want you to tell him to back off.*" He squeezed my leg under the table. "*You're my mate, not his.*"

Sheesh. The males within the bond were overprotective when it came to their females, and it seemed mine was no different, no matter our circumstances. *"Right. I'll get onto that pronto."*

His gaze narrowed on Zayn. *"He believes he can cook for you, and get away with it."*

"Um, last I heard, cooking wasn't a crime."

"Don't make light of my words. He has intentions toward you, and it's completely unacceptable."

"What do you care if he has—"

"Silvie, are you all right?" Zayn took a sip of his orange juice. "If you need a hand to control your warrior, let me know."

"I'm good." I grabbed Guy's hand and hauled him to his feet. "This impossible warrior wants to know the location of my school. Could you lead the way?"

"Sure. You've only got a couple of minutes until the bell. See if you can keep up, Moyer." He stood and zipped away.

Guy 'ported in his wake, and through the dark we traveled. We arrived in a flurry behind a large tree on the perimeter of the school field.

Shoot. They could have traveled a little slower. I clutched my belly as it rolled. "Okay, thanks for that breakneck trip, boys."

"No problem." Zayn eyed me. "I'll catch you for training as we discussed. Hopefully by then, you'll be minus the tag-on."

"The sneaky—" Guy heaved past me, grabbing at Zayn, only he'd 'ported and all Guy got was thin air.

"Okay, you need to chill. You two managed to behave all right in each other's company yesterday."

"Barely, and that's before I knew of his intentions." He gripped my hands and pressed my palms flat on this chest. "I won't have you relying on him, in any way, shape or form."

"What are you doing?" I stared at where the heavy beat of his heart pounded against my flesh. No way. Surely he wasn't— my hands heated and my pulse jumped. It vaulted a second time then beat steadily in time with his. Hell no. He'd aligned our heartbeats as our mated men did in order to strengthen the bond. If I was ever in any distress he'd know, because our hearts would beat in sync. "How could you?"

"It was my choice."

"Are you crazy?"

"Don't fear the change." His grip tightened. "This way I can come in an instant should you need me."

"Aligning our hearts goes deeper than that."

"It's done, and it can't be reversed."

"No, what you've done will only add to your frustration, and mine. In the future you'll feel—" Heck, he'd feel every acceleration in my heartbeat, because it would be mirrored within his. So not good.

He dipped his head to mine. "I know what I'll feel, but it's worth it to know I've seen to your safety. You can wield fire, and as your ability grows and you move through your rising, you'll feel three times its strength. I can't allow you to go through that alone."

"I'm never alone, and my rising could be days or even weeks away. The girls' problem might be solved by then, and us, apart."

"That's irrelevant. You are my mate, and if you ever need me, whether now or at any time in the future, I'll be there."

"Argh." I thumped my forehead against his chest. "You're completely irrational."

"Yes, it comes with being mated, or so I'm discovering." He tipped up my chin and his mouth came down on mine. He took my breath away in a scorching kiss then pulled away. "I'll speak to you later."

"If I speak to you at all, it'll be to give you a blasting." I shoved my shaky hands behind my back. "You'd better leave now before I strangle you."

His gaze searched mine. "You'll 'path me if you need me?"

"No." The last thing I'd ever do was 'path him. I stormed

away.

"Then it's just as well I did what I did."

"Sure it was." Huh, men. I crossed the field toward the path leading to the front of the school. Boy, I needed to calm down. I couldn't let him get to me like this. I inhaled then let out a long breath, hoping it would help. Certainly, the sooner I came up with the answer to the girls' problem and kicked my mate out of my life, the better.

I flicked my hair over my shoulder and marched on. Some students walked in groups, nattering to each other. Others raced ahead to the locker bays. For five years, I'd attended Te Puke High. I had so many friends here, although Faith was the only one who knew of Magio. I passed blocks of two-story high weatherboard-clad classrooms, and eager to get out of their shadow and into the warmth, picked up my already speedy pace. I'd never tried to get to class this quickly.

Inside my locker, I foraged and found the books I needed. The bell pealed loud and clear, and I followed the other students into class. Faith sat at the back, sitting stiffly with a worried look on her face.

She rose and snapped out a blue-gray metal school chair. "What was that all about?"

"You mean on the field?"

"Hell, yes. I wanted to check on you. You and Guy surely know how to…argue."

"What did I say about checking on me, Miss Nosy?" With my elbows on the desk, I plopped forward. "Argh, what am I going to do with him? He stayed in my bed last night."

She gasped and covered her mouth.

"Nothing happened. It was a platonic sleepover. He turned up, and then just didn't leave. Now those feelings I told you about are harassing me big time. I can't feel this way about him."

"You want him?"

I dumped my head into my upturned palms. "Yes, but it's

just the bond which drives him, not a desire for me."

"This is all my fault." She rubbed her forehead on my shoulder. "I'm really sorry. I shouldn't have put you in this position."

"No, it's not your fault, it's Donaldo Wincrest's. He's the one who's about to make the biggest mistake ever."

"Hey." She tugged on my wrist until I lifted my head and looked at her. "I've got your back. We stick together. I'll speak to Guy if you want."

The door to the classroom bumped open and Mrs. Gray tottered in, arms full.

"No, it's better if I deal with him."

She tweaked my chin. "Then cheer up. We'll talk more about this at lunchtime and see if we can gain some more ground on my problem. That way you won't have to see your warrior anymore."

"Yeah, once I fix your problem, it'll fix my own." I straightened as the teacher walked toward me. She was one of my favorite teachers, a kindly older woman, with her salt-and-pepper hair short, straight and styled up higher over her forehead. "Hey, Mrs. Gray."

"Silvie, you missed an important class yesterday." She passed me a stapled set of papers. "With finals so close, I went over some of our previous English exam papers. That one's for you, but it'll have to be homework. Hand it in as quick as you can. Tomorrow would be best."

I slumped onto my desk. Great. I had extra homework, training for a skill I had yet to control, the girls' problem to sort and one very frustrating mate. What a super start to my day.

* * * *

"Aren't you hungry?"

Faith prodded my arm with her elbow.

"I forgot to bring lunch." Ankles crossed, I stared at the yellow leaves of the big tree we'd chosen to lie under at the rear of the school field. Bright, dappled rays beamed through the foliage and washed over us. "There wouldn't have been time with all the bickering between Guy and Zayn anyway."

"You want some of mine?" she mumbled as she took a bite of her ham and cheese sandwich.

I flicked the crumbs off her violet spaghetti strap top, a shirt strikingly similar to one I had. In fact, so were the frayed denim shorts she wore. "Have you been borrowing my clothes again?"

"Yep, but I found these in Hope's wardrobe. She must have borrowed them from you, and now I've borrowed them from her. You'll get them back eventually. Here." She grasped her bag and slung it over. "I've got a donut left over from yesterday's lunch. You know, it's been ages since you made me rocky road."

"It was like last week." I pulled her lunch box out and nabbed the donut, one of the round ones with yellow icing. "So, what should I do about Guy?"

"You need to stop kissing him, and double the marshmallows next time in the rocky road."

"You are so insightful, but he's the one kissing me. You got anything else, oh-so-wise-one?"

"I really like it when you double the nuts too." She smiled as she sat up. "I know. What if you 'path me whenever he turns up? I'll be your go-between."

"I can't keep interrupting you every time I need supervision. I'm not a five-year-old."

"Of course you can. Hold still." She launched to her feet and grabbed a rugby ball before it hit us. She tossed it back to the guys who'd come out to play a game. "Oh, there's Belle. Davio must have thought I needed our empath today."

Belle skipped past the tech building in her skinny white jeans and a pale pink t-shirt. She adjusted her school bag over her shoulder and waved.

"Faith, why don't we bring Belle into the fold? Like me, she'll understand your problem. I could certainly use the help."

"Hmm." She scrunched up her face as she did when in deep thought. "You might be right. I'll run that scenario." Her violet eyes glazed as she focused. "Belle's for peace, not war. I don't see her spilling to Davio or Silas."

"You don't see me spilling what?" Belle plopped onto the ground beside us. "What are you two conspiring to do this time?"

Faith wriggled around on her bottom. "Get ready, because this news is a little nasty, Belle."

During the telling of Faith's forewarning, Belle's face went white. "That's horrendous. Wincrest can't be allowed to do that, and slayers? They're the worst of their warriors." Her gaze jolted to mine. "Who else knows about this?"

"Hope and Guy. That's why Guy's still sticking around. Faith's seen I need his aid on this, and he agreed to help me."

"No, he's helping because of more than that. I'm an empath, remember?"

"If he feels more, it's only because of the bond."

"Yeah, but the bond is also too important to simply toss aside. Deep down, he must recognize it. I certainly wish my mate had the guts to come for me." She shoved her long dark locks over her shoulder.

"I'm sorry, Belle." For her, the loss of her mate had to be incredibly painful.

"I've waited almost two years." She shook her head. "I don't want to toss it aside, but I've no longer got a choice. Sorrell asked me out. I said yes."

"Sorrell?" Faith gripped her hand. "The protector who leads the mountain team? But he's a bear of a man and so aggressive. You two would hardly suit."

"His emotions actually run at an even level, and that's easier for me to process than the huge fluctuations I get around others."

"But Sorrell? He cares for no one. Are you sure?"

"He needs to be shown love to feel it."

"You sound as if you pity him."

She fidgeted with the hem of her pink t-shirt. "Sorrell needs a tender touch, and I can offer him that. My decision is made."

No, the man would stifle Belle's emotions. He was the last person she needed.

"*Are you thinking what I'm thinking?*" Faith muttered in my head.

I didn't doubt I was. I projected my thoughts for her to read, then said, "*We'll work on her next, but one problem at a time.*" Sheesh, this day was just getting worse. Problems abounding everywhere.

"Hey, watch your emotions, Silvie." Belle jerked back. "I'm feeling a touch hot. Maybe I shouldn't have told you about Sorrell, not when you're dealing with enough issues of your own."

"I'm good, Belle. What I can't deal with is the fact Guy aligned our hearts." My blood heated and pulsed at the mere thought of what he'd done this morning. "He's too controlling, and he doesn't listen to a word I say."

"Okay." Belle shuffled back farther. "We really need to change the subject, now. Think cold stuff."

"What I've gotta do is deal with how I'm feeling, and not keep bottling it up."

"No, you need to cool down. We're at school, and there're other students about." Belle pointed to the half-eaten donut in my hand. The icing melted and dribbled. It splattered with a hiss and a spit onto my fingers. "That's more than just a little bottling."

"I had good control over my flare-up last night. I've got this." Only my fingertips blazed red, not yet alight, but looking ready to go. "Oooh, that is so pretty. Maybe I should just go with the flow and consume and burn. That would be so hot."

"No, it wouldn't," Faith growled. "Don't make me 'path

Guy to come and get you out of here. You're dangerously close to losing it."

"Am not." I held up my hands. The red glowed brighter. Oh yeah, perfect. Consume and burn. "It's amazing, isn't it? Look how—"

"Right, 'pathing him now."

"I'm just teasing."

"I'm not."

Belle's cheeks bloomed bright red. "Cold thoughts are your first tactical response to lowering your heat. I know you're enjoying this, but remember what the book said."

"Then let me enjoy it a little—"

"I'm here." Guy stepped out from behind the trunk and jogged toward us. Water sloshed from a pail in his hands. "Faith called."

"Don't you dare even think it!" He was not throwing that at me. I scrambled to my feet, but too late. He dumped the contents over me and steam shot from my hands. "No. They weren't even alight. I had it under control."

He dropped the pail and cupped my cheeks. "What control? Faith said you needed me. Emergency 101."

"101 means it's a non-emergency." I shook my head and icy water flew. "You need to learn your numbers."

Faith chuckled and crossed to me. "Oops, I may have sounded more urgent than I meant. You want me to take you home to change?" She tucked my soggy hair behind my ears.

"No, I have a change of clothes in my locker. You. Come." I seized Faith's hand and dragged her after me.

Belle's giggles traveled on the breeze, and Guy's laughter joined hers.

Oh boy, I was so gonna get him back.

Big time.

* * * *

"There's Zayn." Faith pointed to where he stood leaning

against a tree after the final school bell had rung.

"We're going to train together. Do you wanna come?"

"Nah, homework beckons. Just remember what I said about not spending too much time with him."

"Hey, girls. How was your day?" Zayn pushed off the tree.

"Sunny, except for an odd burst of rain." Faith winked at me, stepped behind the tree and 'ported.

"You want to explain?" he asked.

"Nope." I grabbed his hand. "You need to zap us to that secluded beach spot before my annoying mate turns up. I'm surprised he's not here already."

"I'm onto it. You don't need to tell me twice." He grinned as he 'ported us.

Through the dark we traveled, and then we arrived in the most glorious place on Earth. I twirled with my arms up high. Ahh, the sun blazed down, its heat soaking into my skin and replenishing me. "Fab-u-lous."

"This is the perfect spot for training."

"Is it ever." A forest of pines rose beyond the sand dunes, and dry, wilted grass edged the towering trees. My mouth watered as I ogled all that tinder-dry land. Mmm, a forest full of kindling, just waiting to be set aflame. What a sight that would be. A fire unparalleled to any other would rage. Oh yeah. Within the fire was such beauty, the stunning colors of burnt orange and sizzling red. I loved those colors, but more, I loved the heat. So warm. I wanted to feel—

"Silvie? Where are you going?"

I was off, jogging over the sandy rise.

"Hey, wait. Shoot, there's a blast of heat coming off you."

My fingers itched to light up, and everything within me yearned to burn.

Chapter 6

At my feet the dry grass curled at the tips and blistered.

"Silvie, listen to me." Zayn raced past and came around in front. He shoved up his hands as he hiked it backward. "You've seriously gotta stop."

"No, I've gotta make a fire."

"I know you do, but not like this. We're here for training, not to ignite a forest."

"That's training, just on a larger scale. Why does everyone want to stop me from having fun today?"

"There's fun, and then there's wiping out the home of countless animals and birds."

"Animals?" I staggered to a stop. Birds soared above then dipped to land on the highest branches where they nested. "No, I can't hurt them."

"There's also a camping ground only five miles from here. What happens if people are tramping or exploring these woods?"

I shivered and rubbed my arms, my need to blaze dying a fast death. "Zayn? Take me away from here."

He pulled me into his arms. "You're cool again. That's amazing."

"I mean it. Take me away from here. I don't want to bring about the kind of harm you just said."

"No, we're staying. This is what your training is all about.

Look how quickly you controlled your impulses. Come on. I have an idea." He guided me to the beach, collecting driftwood along the way. Where the dunes provided shelter in a protected area on the sand, he hunkered down and scooped out a hole.

"A fire pit?"

"Yeah, I want to see you make a fire. A small, controlled one." He patted the spot beside him.

"You think I can do it?" I knelt and helped him pile the wood up.

"I know you can. I'm ready whenever you are."

Okay, I could do this. I shook out my hands. Fire. My fingertips warmed and sparked. I touched the dry stringy bark. A tendril of smoke snaked up. Ahh, now this was what I wanted.

"Great." Zayn touched my arm. "Your skin feels warm but not hot. There's no heat wave at all."

"Are you sure? I'm making fire without getting hot?"

"Yes, but that could be because your flame is small, and the source of what you want to burn, minor. Extinguish your fire, and we'll work on something bigger."

I studied the curious seagulls hopping closer. They were beautiful, and this was their home. I wouldn't allow my fire to harm them. The flames at my fingertips spluttered out.

"Perfect." Zayn beamed.

"I did it." I jumped up. "I did it."

He joined me, swung me off my feet. "Congrats."

"You. Did. What?"

Guy's deep voice rumbled from along the beach. He strode toward us. He did not look happy, only I was way too excited to worry about it.

"Hey." I ran and danced around him. "You should have seen what I just did. I controlled my fire and not by cold thoughts, but by not wanting to bring harm. It was so much better."

His frown deepened. "You should have waited for me when

you finished school."

"But I controlled my fire." I grabbed his hands. "Be happy for me."

"You're lucky Faith told me where you were."

"Look." I lugged him to the fire pit and jabbed at the burning wood. "I controlled the fire within me." Couldn't he see what I'd achieved?

"She's got this nailed. There wasn't even any heat coming off her." Zayn scooped sand and tossed it over the fire. It spat and died. "Silvie, we need to extend your training."

"Yes. Yes. Yes."

"She's not doing that with you. Excuse us." Guy held me tight as he 'ported us. We arrived in the stables, and he checked behind him. "Good. He got the point and didn't follow."

"That wasn't very polite."

"Do I look like I care? No." He lifted my arms and wrapped them around his neck, bringing me against him. "I missed you today, and when I find you, it's with him."

"Did you just say you missed me?" Surely not.

"Hell, yes, I missed you." He kissed me, a hot melding that made my temperature rise. Then he tipped me back, kissing me even deeper, until every inch of me warmed for more.

He groaned. "We've gotta stop doing this."

"You started it," I mumbled against his lips. "Although, I'm in complete agreement. We've gotta stop."

"You make me forget. You make me wish for more."

"And you're a terrible influence on me." I ran my finger in a saucy swirl down his chest and over his abs, his wickedly toned abs. He needed to stop working out with a sword, kick back and eat a ton of junk food. Whatever it took, he had to lose this physique that tempted me beyond reason. "Why don't you back up before we both do something we'll regret?"

He caught my finger and brought it to his lips.

"That's not backing up." Which meant it was up to me. I

ducked around him and out into the blinding sunshine.

"Silvie, you can't just walk off." He chased after me.

"Yes, I can." I continued on, firing up my link to Faith. *"Hey, I need a pickup. The outback."*

"Where are you going?"

"Home, and without your help."

"I'm already there, Silvie. I wanted to chat to Hope. We're in her room. Do you see the homestead?"

On the hill, a sprawling earth-toned homestead of clay bricks and mortar proudly stood. It was magnificent in design, three-stories high with a wide wraparound porch. A castle for a king, even though Donaldo Wincrest didn't reside here. *"I see it."*

I cut a path across the baked earth and under a towering stand of eucalyptus trees. A touch of shade cooled my skin from the delicious heat. I picked up my pace to pass out from underneath it. There. Faith and Hope waved from the top corner balcony.

"You can't leave." Guy strode beside me. "We have a problem we need to work on."

"I'll work on it with the girls."

"No, *we'll* work on it with the girls." He pulled me to a stop, and before I could say no, the dark ensued. We arrived on Hope's balcony.

"You have a terrible habit of taking over." And I couldn't let him. I shoved my hair over my shoulder and faced Faith. "From now on I've got to do this on my own. I'm firing my mate. He's off the job. You're with me on that, right?" I couldn't say it any plainer.

Faith struck a wide-eyed look at Guy. "What did you do now?"

"I can't stop kissing her." He opened the glass slider, looking not one bit contrite. "Ladies first."

White lace curtains fluttered against my legs as I stormed

in. How did I get through to him he had to leave? I gripped the smooth, round end post of Hope's New Zealand rimu bed, trying not to tangle my fingers in the white netting trickling from the canopy. "He also said he missed me. This really isn't working out the way it should."

"Then we'll sort this problem fast." Faith plopped onto the bed. "Between the four of us, we'll come up with an answer."

Hope squeezed my shoulder. "I'll do what I can to help."

Guy settled on the corner settee padded in blue velvet. "I've got an idea. Since I'm here to aid Silvie, what better way than with my skill? I have a spell which can loosen subconscious thoughts so they come to the forefront of the mind." He leaned forward, elbows to his knees as he eyed me. "You want to give it a go?"

"Is it safe?"

"I'd never place your life in danger. Only you will see the thoughts you release." He held out a hand. "Let's try it."

I plodded across the room and joined him on the settee. I was game. We needed a resolution, and fast. "How does this work?"

"Simply look into my eyes." He took my hands. "And relax."

"Then don't look at me too intensely and I might." I faced him, touching my knees to his.

"I'm sorry I've made things more difficult for you. It was never my intention." The silver rimming the blue of his eyes swirled to life. "Are you ready?"

"Like yesterday."

"Then let's begin." He stroked my palms with his thumbs. "My mate, within your mind and hidden deep, is an answer only you must seek. Dislodge and release, send it spinning free, allow it to ride and think only of thee."

My stomach rolled and pitched. Or was that my head? I toppled forward.

"I've got you." He caught me. "Close your eyes. It'll help."

As I did the dark embraced me. Memories spun, a mirage of pictures rolling one after the other, all flinging backward through time. Finally they slowed then dripped past until only one remained.

The rain had finally cleared. Faith's mother Kate had bundled us girls up in our winter coats and walked us to the park. At six, our energy was boundless. Faith had raced ahead and clambered up the steps of the rocket slide. She made the top rung then shuffled onto her bottom.

I ran toward her with a giggle, almost sliding over in the soggy grass. "There's a puddle. You're gonna get so dirty."

"No, I won't. Come up." She rocked back and forth. "If we go down together, we'll go so fast, we'll miss the puddle and zing right off the end."

"Nah-ah." Cold muddy water with insects flying over top. Ick. Not for me. "I don't like getting wet."

"Scaredy-cat." Tongue poked out, she shoved her thumbs in her ears and twiddled her fingers.

"I'm not scared, and you better hurry before your mum comes."

"I'm already here." Kate rushed in. "What do you think you're doing, Faith? We came for the swings."

"Okay, I'm coming down." Faith laughed as she pushed off. Her coat snagged on something and she squealed. She toppled forward and rolled down. "Mum-mie."

Kate dashed forward, but Faith plowed off the end and landed in the middle of the puddle. Mucky water sprayed everywhere.

"Help." Faith half-laughed, half-cried as she slapped at the water.

Kate juggled her camera, accidentally taking a shot as she tossed it by the strap over her shoulder.

"I'm closer. I'll help her." I edged around the grassiest side of the puddle and leaned a hand in. "Don't pull. I'll pull you."

"I promise I won't." She slapped her hand into mine and muck oozed between our fingers. "You're like the best friend ever."

"You're like the worst." I heaved her out.

"We stick together." She hugged me, coating me in the sloppy mud.

Ah, what a moment. I couldn't help smiling at the long ago memory. From that day on, we'd always said those words to each other. We stick together. That's when it had all begun.

"Silvie?"

Guy shook my shoulders.

"Wake up."

I stretched and opened my eyes, finding myself cradled in his lap. "That was a blast from the past."

Faith and Hope knelt on the snowy white carpet next to us. Faith took my hand and rubbed the back against her cheek. "Are you all right? You've been out for ages."

"Yeah, but best of all I know what I need to do."

"Really?"

"Yep, we've been best friends since forever. We've always been there for each other. When we were six, we made the promise to stick together. We even shook on it."

She gasped. "The slide. The puddle."

"That's the one. From then on, we've always had each other's back."

"But how does that memory fix the problem? You and me sticking together isn't anything new."

"Think about it. We've always stuck together, and where it counts." This was why she needed my help, and I couldn't let her down. "Dralion is where the problem exists, and Dralion is where it counts. We haven't stuck together there."

"Are you saying—" She jerked back. "No. There isn't a chance—I won't expose you to Donaldo. You're not stepping one foot on Dralion soil."

"I don't like the idea either, but—"

"No. I said, no!"

"We had a deal."

"One we brokered as children."

"You want to cancel it?"

"No, but you can't ask this of me."

"I think I already did." I held out my hand. "Let's shake on it again. Deal?"

Chapter 7

"I can't believe this." Hope staggered to her feet. "No Peacian is allowed in Dralion. It just can't happen with the dome blocking them."

Guy shifted underneath me. "I never thought this would be your answer. If I had, I wouldn't have spelled you."

"It's the only answer." Why would no one listen to me?

"You can't go to Dralion. Like Faith, I won't allow it."

"You don't have a choice. I'm the key, and no one else."

"It's too dangerous for you. In fact, I'll fix this now." His enchanter eyes swirled to life.

"Don't you dare." He was going to turn back time, or something else to make me forget. I clamped a hand over his face. "You are not allowed to enchant me in order to get your own way."

He plucked my fingers free and glared. "It's my right to protect you, and if I believe you're about to do something to bring harm to yourself, I'll change the course of events."

"You have no right to, not when you gave your rights away."

"Then I'll take them back."

"Whoa. No, you won't." I had to get out of here before he acted on those irrational thoughts. I shuffled off his lap and onto my feet.

"Where are you going?"

"Home." I grabbed Faith's hand. "Please, take me out of here before he does something idiotic. We stick together, even if you don't like it."

"Argh. I might just cancel that deal after all." She struck a look at Hope. "Sorry, I've gotta get her home. We'll chat later, okay?"

"Later."

Guy stepped up to me. "You'll stay out of trouble, or I will follow."

"Faith, now." I needed distance from him.

She edged between us. "Guy, let's all take a breather. I'll talk to her, I promise. I'm not brokering a new deal." She flashed us away.

We arrived in my bedroom, and thankfully Guy didn't follow. "Phew. He's too persistent for his own good."

"I know you said he's driven by the bond to see to your welfare, and I don't argue against that, but there's more. While you were out of it, I saw how much he cared and that emotion goes deeper than what you realize."

"It's still the bond. He wanted to spell me so his part in all this was done."

"You don't want to be with him?"

"I can't. We'd never be able to make it work. He's a warrior." And his first instinct was to let me go. He had, and we'd released each other.

"It'll be okay." She hugged me. "Take some time to calm down, and by the way, you have to come up with another way to solve my problem, one that doesn't involve you going to Dralion. That won't work for any of us."

"All roads lead to Dralion. Wincrest creates the problem, and he's the one who needs to be swayed. I can't do that from here."

She knocked her knuckles against my forehead. "Yep, still

hard."

"My head has to be to keep up with you."

"Thanks. You sound just like my—" She clapped a hand over her mouth. "Oh, my mum. I clear forgot. I'm supposed to help her with dinner. She's adapting to Dralion, which means she's commandeered an area in the kitchens just for herself. Having her own space to cook helps her feel a little more like she never left home. I promised I'd be there."

"Then go." Kate couldn't leave Dralion, just as I couldn't get in. Ahh, now that might be my answer. I could get in if…

"Thanks, Silvie. If you need me, 'path, otherwise I'll see you at school tomorrow. We'll try and figure something out then."

This was my chance. I had to catch a ride with Faith, and one too late for her forewarning to activate on. The dome room was the only portal in and out. Only warriors and Wincrests had the image and access through it.

"Yep, at school." I waved as she shimmered then grabbed hold of her. Oh hell, now I'd done it. She 'ported, and with me barely hanging on. *Please don't change your course. Please don't change your course.* It was near impossible once a 'porter left, and only if enough time existed to alter their coordinates. Hopefully, she hadn't had enough of that.

I shut my eyes against the dark since I couldn't know the layout of their dome room. If I did, I'd be a threat Wincrest would never allow free if this all went to crap.

My feet hit a slippery surface.

Faith screeched. "Holy moly, Silvie. Why'd you do that?" She slammed her hands over my eyes even though they were tightly shut. "Hell, we're the only ones in here. You're damn lucky."

Moldy air had me gagging for a breath. "It stinks in here. Could you hurry it through? Perhaps your bedroom would be best."

"What were you thinking, catching a ride like that?"

"Have you had forewarning I shouldn't have since we left?"

"No, but—"

"My being here must be right then."

"You being here is insane. Guy will go berserk when he hears."

"Then we won't tell him, and my being caught would be insane. Move it, now."

"What I should do is take you home." Her hand was hot against my eyes, and getting sweatier by the second.

"I'm here now, and I can't get out of Dralion unless you bring me back through this—this place. So, we're all good provided I don't get caught. Like right now. Really, move it. I don't wanna get caught." My heartbeat pounded in my ears.

"Okay. We'll do it your way, because damn it, I can't deny there's still no forewarning. Hold on."

I swayed against her as she 'ported us again, a quick spurt this time.

"We're here."

I wobbled and fell onto my bottom. The room was dark and my heartbeat still thumped like thunder. Nice way to ensure my ticker worked well. "You got a light?"

"One sec."

"*Silvie?*" Guy's voice rang inside my head. "*Your heart's beating too fast. Where are you?*"

"*Bedroom.*"

"*I'm already in your bedroom and you're not here.*"

"*I didn't mean my bedroom.*"

"*What have you done?*"

"*Um, nothin' much.*" My mate was like a bloodhound.

Faith flicked on the overhead light and I did a double take. Wow. Her room was massive, far bigger than any one person needed. I slipped around on the polished wood flooring as I crawled to her giant canopied bed. I had to calm my heartbeat.

Guy would flip if I didn't. Oh, pretty bed. Focusing on the stunning violet silk bed cover with detailed mauve and gold stitching helped. Using the bedpost, I heaved myself up.

"Whose bedroom then?"

"Does it matter? I can visit anyone's bedroom I like. Anyway, I can't talk right now. I'm busy trying to relax. And you're not helping."

"Why can't you talk?"

I spun around as his voice rumbled from the other side of Faith's door.

"See," Faith whispered madly, her gaze darting back and forth between me and the door. "He cares."

"Is it because you're in here?" He rapped loudly on the solid paneled wood.

"You are such a pest." I marched to the door and yanked it open. "One who needs to get a life, and preferably where you're not pestering me."

"You're in Dralion." He stalked in, his voice ragged and the silver in his eyes hardening to a steely gray.

"So perceptive."

He pulled me hard against him, his heart beating a rapid tattoo against mine. "What if a warrior had seen you?"

"Well, ah, that didn't happen. Faith would have had forewarning," I mumbled into his silky shirtfront, the color as dark as his mood.

Faith shut the door and flicked the lock. "Which could only mean, and I hate to say this, Guy, but Silvie's meant to be here."

"See, all is good," I pointed out.

"Nothing is good, Silvie. You're a Peacian. In Dralion." His hold on me tightened. "This palace is Donaldo's domain, and he knows all who reside within its walls."

"I'm here, and I'm staying." I planted my hands on his chest and pushed, trying to gain some space. My attempt was futile. "I can't fix Faith's problem from anywhere else. You know it, and I know it."

"Did you see the dome room?"

"Nope. I kept my eyes shut, but I'd like to see the warriors' barracks if I'm not to stay here. Do you have your own room?"

"I do, not that you're staying there. If anyone spotted you, they'd believe us together."

"I'll be a family member. A cousin perhaps?"

"My only cousins are far-removed, and from an adopted line."

"Oh, I have an idea." Faith raced into her dressing room then reappeared with an armload of clothes. Within the bundle was an assortment of leather pants and button-down shirts in black and white. "You could be a new recruit, not yet a warrior, but one in training."

"She cannot stay in the barracks. She shouldn't even be here." Guy shoved a hand through his tousled black hair.

"I'll be your far-removed cousin who's a new recruit. Will that work so we can share a room?" I didn't care to be on my own.

"Damn. I guess." His look was incredulous. "And that was not my agreement."

"I think it was, and remember we need to move on this problem."

"We really do." Faith tossed the clothing onto the bed and rummaged through it. From the pile, she pulled out a duffel bag and a pair of black boots, ones that looked lethal with silver spikes protruding from the sides and the tips.

"Ew, that's nasty."

"You'll need them if you want to blend in."

Guy gripped my shoulders. "Which also means you can't use your fire skill here. It'll cause major problems if anyone sees it. Donaldo would be all over you in a second."

"So you agree I can stay?"

"It looks like I don't have a choice, but there will be

conditions."

"I agree. Silvie needs conditions." Faith packed some of the clothing into the bag. "Yours is one of the greatest of the battle skills. Keeping it hidden is a must."

"Guy already said that, and I'll take every precaution."

Guy nabbed the packed duffel from Faith and slung it over his shoulder. "I should not be agreeing to this. I don't wish to live with my mate and allow our relationship to deepen."

"C'mon, cousie." I playfully nudged him in the arm. "It's all good." Or as good as it could be now I was on enemy soil.

Faith pulled me into a tight hug. "I wish you could stay here with me, but Donaldo would become suspicious. The staff talk."

"Don't worry about it. Guy won't let any harm come to me."

"That's damn right." He grasped my hand, his gaze on Faith. "We'd better leave while the going's good. I'll see you later."

"Look after her."

"Will do." He flashed us away and into his room in a blink.

The warriors' barracks. The one place I'd never expected to visit. His room. Two single wooden-slatted beds covered with thin mattresses took up most of the space. So barren. Even the walls, painted a dull gray, remained unadorned. "Nice digs you've got."

"There's a bathroom to the side, but this is just a place where I rest my head." He propped the duffel on top of a tall chest crammed into the corner. He unpacked the contents into the top drawer then folded the canvas bag and slid it under the gap between the floorboards and the base. "Are you hungry? I can grab something from the dining room. There's food out most of the time."

"No, I don't feel like eating." Faith hadn't been kidding when she'd said I'd been out of it for ages. Through the window the night sky was dark, although glimmering with thousands of stars. I eased onto one of the single beds and kicked off my shoes.

"I should say welcome to my home, except I wish you weren't here." He lifted my legs and tipped me back. He sat, propped my feet in his lap and massaged them.

"Why, thanks for having me over, cousie." I stretched and tucked his lumpy pillow under my head.

"You've been trouble since the moment I met you." He crawled in beside me, almost rolling me off the bed.

"Hey, this bed was made for one."

"We need to discuss our relationship."

"You can do that from the other bed."

"Inside this room, you're my mate." He rubbed his cheek against mine. "Just so we're clear."

"And just so you're clear." My bottom hung off the side as I rolled and faced him. "You're a bed-hog is what you—"

He kissed me, long and with wicked skill. My head spun under the onslaught. Oh my, my mate surely knew how to kiss. When he let me come up for air, I grabbed in a lungful before his mouth once again claimed mine.

"Trouble," I mumbled against his lips as I pushed my hands deep into his glorious hair. It was beautiful, silky and the darkest shade I was coming to adore.

Slowly, he pulled back. "I'm lucky to have met you."

"Hey, luck had nothing to do with it." I tapped his lower lip. "It's all Faith's fault. She's the reason I ended up in the outback, and she's the reason I'm now hanging out here with you."

"She has a lot to answer for." He stroked the back of my head, his eyes ablaze with the enchanter's silver. "Although, I can't imagine having never met you, or missing this chance to forge some lasting memories. I'm glad for that, if nothing else."

I tucked my cheek against his chest and snuggled. "I'm kinda glad too."

"We'll fix this problem." His chest rose on a deep

inhalation.

"You bet we will." I yawned and closed my eyes. "Tomorrow."

He wrapped his arms around me, holding me close. "To sticking together."

I drifted, all cozy and content. This felt so right, in his arms.

* * * *

"Silvie, wake up."

I stretched and rubbed my bare feet against his warm socked ones. Underneath me, the bed shifted. No. Not the bed. Guy wriggled, and hell, I was lying on top of him.

Pushing to my elbows, I found myself eye to eye with the most bewitching sight. Oh my goodness. He looked rumpled and eat 'em up delicious with stubble shadowing his jaw.

"I'm awake." I leaned in and kissed him, unable to help myself.

"So am I, and we'd better move or else dangerous things will happen." He rolled us out of the bed in one swift move.

I tip-toed my fingers down his chest. "Oooh, Dralion. Do you feel the danger?"

"Most definitely." He trapped my hand under his. "Let's plan. First, you keep the name Silvie, but take my last name of Moyer. The adopted side goes by it."

"Okay, so I'm like Silvie, um, Moyer?" That was a little weird.

"Yes." He smiled then abruptly straightened his mouth. "Grab some of Faith's clothes. The bathroom's that way." He turned me by the shoulders and gave me a nudge toward the dresser.

I opened the drawers and pulled out what I needed, a pair a black leather pants and a black shirt. Holding them to my chest, I turned, and wow. Out the window was nothing but one massive ocean. It was as if we sat right on the precipice of a cliff, with only the air we breathed between us and doom.

I stumbled to the window and grasped the sill. Below, the sheer edge of a black granite cliff-face plummeted two-hundred feet. At the base, waves crashed hard and sprayed high. No wonder only stars had been viewable last night.

Guy hemmed me in, his hands planted on either side of the sill. "It's The Great Orbiting Ocean. Dralion's palace is located right on the cliffs that run unbroken for ninety miles in each direction. The energy field extends over us and the ocean."

"The granite is solid, right?"

"Yes, and this palace has stood for hundreds of centuries. I can guarantee the cliffs won't fail us now."

I flattened my back against him. "Well, I guess you've got a nice unobstructed view."

"You're safe." His breath tickled my cheek and fluttered my hair across my face.

"I'd never question that with you." I looked over my shoulder at him then popped a kiss on his cheek.

He drew in a haggard breath then lifted one arm. "Scoot."

I ducked under it and scurried to his bathroom.

It was tiny, and once I shut the door, one step in either direction had me against a wall. I shucked my clothes and squeezed into the shower cubicle then flicked on the brass lever. Water gushed out and smacked me in the face. Okay, good water pressure, and a nice wake-up call.

I spat out the mouthful and scrubbed myself from head to toe.

After drying, I jiggled into the leather pants and zipped them up. I tucked the loose-sleeved black shirt on over top.

I opened the door a crack and peered out. "Guy, do you have a spare toothbrush?"

He stood at the window, now wearing tight black jeans, and oh yeah, the denim rounded his butt with infinite precision. Rolling up the sleeves of his tan shirt, he crossed the room and eased past me. "There should be one in the bottom drawer." He hunkered down in front of the slim-line vanity and foraged. When he stood up, he had a brush and a razor in hand. "Here you go."

"Thanks." I brushed my teeth as he patted suds over his jaw. "This feels rather domesticated. Are you going to shave?"

"Sure am." He ran the razor in a nice long stroke along his skin.

"You're getting suds in your hair." I lifted it free where it curled onto his nape. Our gazes clashed in the oval mirror on the wall. "I'm an incredibly helpful cousin."

He smiled. "My mother used to hold my father's hair when he shaved, for the exact same reason."

"You miss them, don't you?"

"I wish my mother had never died. I was so young, and the memories so few." He set his razor down and patted his face dry with a towel. "My father though, I'll see him again, as soon as I've freed him."

My chest tightened, and his pain seared me as if it were my own. "I'm sorry your father is locked away. You have neither of them, and I hold the one item that belonged to your mother." My throat clogged, but I pushed on and withdrew his mother's ring from around my neck.

"Don't." He shoved up a hand.

"No, you've kept your word to her and given it to me, and now it's my turn to give it back. I never knew your mother, but I'm sure she would have wanted you to have this. I can give it back. It's mine to do with as I wish."

A tear pooled in the corner of his eye and trickled down his cheek. "You hold the other half of my soul, and she was right when she told me to give it to you." He took the necklace and slid it back over my head. "Thank you, but the fact you now have it, means more than if I did."

"Are you sure? Because I'd give it back to you in a heartbeat."

"I know you would." He pressed me against the wall and kissed me, his mouth deliciously warm over mine. All too soon, he pulled away. "I lose track of my thoughts when I'm around you. Let's get out of here. I'll show you the areas where you're permitted, although not without me."

Striding for the door, he tugged me along. "Guy, no. We're cousins."

"Damn. Forgot. No hand-holding, I guess." He let go and opened the door. "Cousins first."

I edged into the darkened passageway. Talk about gloomy. Doorways were recessed into textured walls of near black. Wall lighting flickered eerily between every other doorway on alternate sides. "And the place just gets better."

"Shh." He shut the door and gripped my shoulder. "Warriors come and go. This is our domain. Always watch what you—"

Three warriors rounded the far corner and stormed toward us. The man at the front of the pack had oily black hair hanging over his shoulders, and he wore a vest of brown leather. Tattoos of fire-breathing dragons curled one over the other on his bare chest and arms, and on a leather belt hanging low on his hips, a roughened metal mallet dangled. Whoa. Daunting.

The man striding beside him was as intimidating, his brown scraggly hair covering one half of his face, and a singular spiked piercing glinted in his visible ear. His biceps bulged as he balled his fists around not one, but two swords at his sides. Okay, why did Faith not give me a sword? Even a dagger right now would be good. Well, I could just kick him with my spiky boots if the warrior made a move.

The two men stopped, eyeing me as a warrior woman walked around them and halted in front. "Who are you?" she demanded.

I cleared my throat but couldn't find my voice. The woman looked scary. She had one half of her head shaved on either side, giving her a mohawk of bright red. A piece of coiled silver pierced one nostril, and round silver hoops looped through her eyebrows. Along with the tightest of battle leathers, she too had a sword sheathed at her side. Okay, so I had Guy. I slid against him, relishing his closeness.

"I said who are you?"

"Silvie." I also had the fire skill, and even though I couldn't use it, I had to toughen up.

"Xrnina, this is my cousin, Silvie Moyer. Silvie, these are three of our leading eight. Xrnina, Killian and Abelard."

I shivered. The two men, slayers, were the ones who'd soon court Faith and Hope. Yeah, thanks, Faith. Lovely of you to dump this problem on me. "Hey."

"*I'm here. I won't let anyone hurt you.*" Guy's fingers dug into my shoulder, though his gaze remained on the others. "Silvie is a new recruit, and yet to come into her rising. She's excited to see what we do, to decide whether being a warrior is for her."

Killian crossed his arms and planted his feet wide. "Moyer, eh? Is there any possibility she'll be an enchanter as you are?"

"No. If she had that skill it would already be evident in her eyes. The silver rim foretells the skill to come."

"Of course. There is only you and your father, but I had hoped. Carry on." Done with the conversation, the man walked off and the other two followed. They disappeared around the corner.

"How can you stand being around them?" I whispered. "They lead so many teams onto Peacian soil. They kill, and ruthlessly."

"With the war, there is bloodshed. Both nations fight."

"No. Peacians defend against warrior attacks. We can't get onto your land."

"Which is exactly why we'll never see eye to eye. Enemies, even though soul-bound." He marched off, and with no choice, I trekked after him.

Stupid mated bond. What power that be ever thought he and I should be mated, needed a good talking to. "Guy, wait up. You're not personally my enemy."

"I know." He slowed, and then stopped in front of two swinging doors. He glanced through the top square glass panel of one. "We're here. Don't speak to anyone unless I give you the okay."

"Gladly." I didn't want to communicate with these people anyway.

He held open the door and I snuck in. Two dozen trestle tables packed out the dining hall. Warrior men and woman sat in full training gear, their swords glinting from their sides.

Shuddering, I opened our link. *"Okay, so why are they all so quiet? That's highly abnormal for this many people in one room."*

"They're speaking, just in hushed tones since most of us hold the advanced senses."

"Protectors don't worry about that. They just turn their receptors down so they can hear as they please."

"We lower our voices instead. It's called practice, for when we're out in the field. It's all about stealth."

"Of course. I should have thought of that." Everything they did probably pertained to training.

"Lead the way to the servery. We'll draw attention to ourselves if we don't move." He waited one step behind.

"Shouldn't you go first? I'm just the recruit."

Guy pressed on my lower back. *"That would be the custom, except I wish to guard your back."*

"Because…"

"You don't fast-heal, and it's not unusual for a warrior to test a new recruit on their first day out."

"As in 'toss-a-dagger' test? Lovely bunch, aren't you?"

"Stop stalling and start moving."

"If a dagger comes my way, you're welcome to step in its path."

"You talk too much."

"You hover too much."

"Must you always argue?" He nudged me along.

"Absolutely. Where's the fun in life, if you don't?" I walked to the servery. No turning back. I was here, and I had a job to do, roomful of warriors included.

An array of food waited in deep metal dishes. Steam curled from the bacon and sausages, releasing a heavenly aroma. Potato hash overflowed the next dish, and kitchen staff topped up the last platter of scrambled eggs. At least I didn't have to worry that Guy wasn't eating well.

He passed me a plate and leaned in to my ear. "One day, we should have a meal on our own, just the two of us. We haven't done that yet." He eased back. "There's toast, cold cereals and fruits farther down if that's what you'd prefer."

"No, this looks good. Hold out your plate." I loaded our plates with the hot offerings.

He munched on a hash brown. "Do you have a favorite place to eat? You know, on…"

Why was he asking me that? "Ah, you sound suspiciously like you're asking me out."

"No." He scratched his head. "I'm just curious."

"Well, stop with the curiosity." I side-stepped to the toast, buttered two slices and then added one to each of our plates.

He brushed against me. "Dralion's beaches are predominantly black sand. They hold such heat. You'd like them."

"Are you trying to tempt me?" Because boy, he might with that kind of comment.

"Maybe." He took my plate along with his. "We'll sit with Vitaria. She's a new recruit too."

He led the way to the far corner where it was quietest. That totally suited me. We approached a young woman. Her white-blond hair was cut into a short bob, the ends flicking softly out. She jiggled in her chair as she spotted Guy. "Hey, you're back. You said you'd be in the outback this morning."

"I had a change of plans." Guy edged onto the wooden bench and set our plates down. "Vitaria, meet Silvie Moyer. She's testing the waters like you are. Silvie, Vitaria."

"Hi." I sat, keeping to the other side of Guy.

"Nice to meet you." She beamed and reached out a hand, the short dagger sheathed at her wrist nicking her skin.

"Um, you should watch that." I ignored her hand, but pointed at the blade.

She followed my gaze. "Oh, I keep forgetting to pick up a new casing from supplies. Thanks." She unstrapped the blade and set in on the table. "So, a Moyer? Are you related to Guy?"

"His cousin. A fourth or fifth." Grinning, I knocked my shoulder against Guy's. "We played together as kids."

"Don't let your food get cold." Guy poured a glass of milk from the jug on the table then set it in front of me. "Drink that too. It's good for you."

"Did I say cousin? I meant Dad." And since our people didn't physically age past our eighteenth year, not a gray hair or a wrinkle, I could easily run with that scenario.

"It's cousin, and rein in your—"

"Playfulness?"

"Behavior."

"You are one very strict cousin, but one I adore sparring with." I scooped a spoonful of eggs and ate. "So, what's it like being a newbie, Vitaria?"

"I was shaking when I first arrived, but Guy took me under his wing. Things are better now I'm more relaxed. I'll help show you around if you like." She bit into her toast smeared with butter and jam.

"Ah, right." I eyed Guy. *"Why's she being so nice?"*

"Many of the warriors are. We're just people who care about our country and want the best for all those who live in it."

"You would think that."

He squeezed my leg under the table. *"You like me, right?"*

"You're different."

"Vitaria has a twin brother. You two actually have a lot in common."

"That won't make us buddy-buddies. So, where is her brother? Is he a recruit too?"

"No, her brother's unskilled. He remains at home caring for their mother. She's very ill, and the healers have said it may be terminal." He stroked my leg.

"So, she's like the breadwinner of the family?"

"Yes. Her father was my father's best friend, and they were both captured together." He glanced at Vitaria as she spoke to someone on the other side of her. *"It's why I've taken her under my wing. She doesn't have anyone here, and she remains unmated. She needs someone to lean on."*

"Don't even think it." I clenched his hand, hating his insinuation. She might be an unmated warrior, but she couldn't have my man. *"She can't be the one. I don't want a visual of who you end up with."*

He speared his bacon and ate. *"The same applies to you. Agree with me that Zayn is out."*

"You don't fight fair."

"I don't want to fight at all."

"All right, I agree." I shoved a forkful of sausage into my mouth, giving him the answer he wanted. If he had the same emotions storming though him as I did, then I couldn't deny him that request. Damn, what a stupid, senseless bond.

Chapter 8

"Where are they going?" I leaned into Guy's side as warriors dispersed from the dining room in large groups.

"Training. It's the first order of business after breakfast. There's an outdoor arena next to these barracks."

Back home, our protectors did the same, and then they followed orders, heading out to guard our villages and the locations which saw the most attacks by warriors infiltrating our shores. Our lucrative diamond and gold mines were constantly hit, and so too, our coal reserves and forests.

Warriors came and they took, and here I was sitting amongst them, not raising a hand. This sucked, in a hundred different ways. Still, I deposited my plate and cutlery into the cleaning trays beside the servery and plodded after Guy and Vitaria.

Vitaria chatted a mile a minute with Guy. It was a relief when we arrived at the supplies room and she stopped to consider which sheath would go best with her blade. Done, we continued on. At the end of the long passageway we came out into an open-aired arena. It was massive, with its ancient architecture and circular dusty floor sprinkled with sand. Blocked seats, layered back and up, towered three-stories high. Impressive, and close in size to our arena in Peacio. This place would hold thousands of spectators, but for now, warrior men and woman trained with their swords and spears and axes, with shields and headgear worn for protection. Some had changed into red tunics with leather-flapped skirts, and they lunged and parried, as accurate with their brutally sharp weapons as any protector would be. If Silas and Davio knew I was here right now, they'd freak.

I stepped past two battling men. One of the men's blades struck flesh and bone, and blood spurted in a wide arc. Yuck. I hurried along, catching up to Guy.

He and Vitaria had found a clear spot. Guy slid his headgear on then gripped the hilt of his blade. "Silvie, Vitaria looks all gentle and unassuming, but she knows exactly how to fight. Stay back."

"Right, out of the way." I leaned against the safety railing.

Vitaria pulled her sword free and rested it between her hands, the blade flat across both palms as she eyed Guy. "We fight, and no attempting to distract."

"When you're ready." Guy bowed then whipped around. His sword slashed down on Vitaria's as she moved like lightning to meet his attack.

Whoa. I scurried under the railing and into the first row of seats.

"Silvie?"

Zayn's voice bounced inside my head.

"Hey."

"I can take you to school if you'd like."

"Ah, I'm going to have to skip today. I've got another project on."

"Do you need a hand?"

"No, I'm all good."

"Well, if you change your mind, 'path me."

"I will. Catch ya later."

I shut the link as Guy dove in for a second attack. His tan shirt pulled tight over his back, molding to muscle. Yep, all was definitely good. They both moved, their swords clashing and meeting dead center. Guy breathed roughly and Vitaria eyeballed him, and then they fought with a torrent of energy. Sweat poured off them as their morning session progressed.

All around, dozens of warriors fought equally as hard, skillfully, and with dedication. It was no wonder when we fought them we never knew who would win. Sometimes we came out on top, and at other times, they did.

"Silvie."

I spun around, came eye to eye with Hope. "What are you doing here?"

"Shh." She pressed her finger against her lips. "Faith sent me. She's at school, but since I was already here, she asked me to get you somewhere safe."

"What? Why somewhere safe?"

Her gaze darted toward Guy. "She had another forewarning."

"Not again." She had to stop having those, and I was going to insist on it.

"Just come," she urged, tugging me along. "And don't draw any attention to yourself."

"I am having a word with her."

"You and me both." She pulled me past the seating on the lower level and through a small gap between two rows which dipped down into a darkened corridor. "This is the way out, to the palace grounds."

"No way. That's one place I'm not allowed."

"Well, the stables, right next to the palace. I've got two horses ready to ride since neither of us can 'port."

"To ride where?"

"Where you can't burn everything down."

"Are you saying—" We burst out of the corridor and into the sultry sunlight. "Oooh, nice."

"You're about to explode. Now get moving."

"Please tell me you don't mean explode the way I would mean explode?"

"*Silvie? Where are you?*"

It was Guy, and no surprise since my heart was trying to leap from my chest.

"*The bathroom.*"

"*Grrr, don't lie to me. I can sense that through our link.*"

"*The outdoors. It's a lovely day and all. I'm taking a walk. Well, actually a run. I need the exercise. Just ask Faith.*"

"*Stop being evasive.*"

"Silvie, hurry." Hope yanked me around a corner and toward a stable hand who waited with two mares. She hoisted herself into the saddle.

"*I mean it, Silvie. Where the hell are you? You just can't up and disappear like this.*"

"*I'm with Hope. Apparently we're taking a ride. Nothing for you to worry about.*" If I was about to blow, I didn't want him in the firing line.

"*You're at the stables?*" He shimmered into sight.

Drat. He was too fast for his own good. "As it appears, yes."

"Where you go, I go." He bent and cupped his hands. "Here, mount up."

I set my foot in his clasp and he lifted me. The leather creaked as I settled into place. "Faith said I'm about to explode. She sent Hope to take me to a safe place."

He flicked a look Hope's way. "How bad will it be?"

"Faith never said, only to hurry and make sure we're far enough away so no one sees. She gave me the perfect spot."

He leapt up behind me and grasped the reins. Bending low, he prodded the horse with his knees and we were off. "Hold on tight."

We rode out the main gates after Hope. We veered left toward the forest path. Pine trees grew tall and strong either side as we galloped. Above, the thick canopy masked the sun, but the ocean and its rhythmic crashing reached me on the breeze. The rough path narrowed as we followed Hope's lead.

I ducked my head as tree branches snagged my hair and clothing. Guy bent lower, squishing me into the saddle. "Since you're now here, you could 'port us."

"It appears Hope knows where to go, but I'll zap us if I need to."

"I don't want her hurt. Make her leave once we get there."

"We're almost there," Hope called over her shoulder.

We rode into the sunshine. The black granite cliffs appeared in a deadly drop. Whoa.

Hope reared around and pulled her horse to a stop. "This is where Faith said to come."

Guy tugged the reins and his horse halted beside hers. "You go. I can handle her heat."

The wind lifted her blond hair and swept it about her face. She shoved it back and eyed me. "Faith's instructions were to go with the flow, and don't fight the fall."

"Don't fight the fall?" I gulped, so hard my throat hurt. "Ooo-kay. Thanks for that."

She nudged her horse's flanks then rode away.

Guy dismounted, gripped my hips and lifted me clear of the horse. He clapped the mare on its rear. It bolted and raced after Hope into the woods.

"Right, don't fight the fall." I stalked toward the cliff's edge. Below, the ocean stirred, the depths of darkest blue tinged with white caps. "I can't believe I'm about to explode when I've been controlling my skill of late."

"Your skill is still gaining in strength." He eased in behind me and stroked my arms.

"Hey, not so close, Guy. You've got to be careful too."

He rested his chin on the top of my head, and rubbed as if trying to soothe me. "I need to remain close. I won't let you fall, no matter what Faith said."

Of course he wouldn't. He was my mate and our bond pulsed strongly. I squeezed his hands then dragged his arms around me. I needed him too, even though I shouldn't give in to that need. "You would make the best boyfriend. That's if you weren't a warrior."

"I can't change who I am."

"I'd never ask you to." The sun glinted along the horizon. "I never thought this would happen."

"What would happen?" His lips whispered across my cheek, so soft.

"That I'd like you this much, to the point where I don't want to give you up."

"That's how you feel?" He held perfectly still.

"Truthfully, yes." I couldn't lie to him. Didn't even want to.

He dragged in a deep breath. "Hell, since we're being honest. I never thought I'd begin falling for you either."

"You mean that?" Please, please mean it.

"Yes, not that I can do a damn thing about it."

"Then we're still ending things?"

"Yes, even though every hour that passes means an hour less with you."

"This is such a mess." Goodness, why were we putting ourselves through this? I pulled away in an attempt to be the responsible one.

"Don't." He grabbed my hand. "I lost my mother at such a young age, but at least I knew her. The same goes with you. I wouldn't trade the time we've had together for anything in the world. We need to store the good memories, and appreciate them for what they are."

"You're saying the good memories will sustain us?"

"Yes." He raked a hand through his hair. "Or they better."

"This is still a mess." I stormed away then kicked the craggy edge, mad and frustrated. A flare of heat coursed through my veins, pulsing and building. Damn it. I hated that I'd miss him once this was all done.

"Silvie, look at me."

I swung around. Flames flared to life at my fingertips. "Just back off. This is my battle, not yours."

His wide-eyed gaze shot to my feet. "Hell, you're melting the rock."

"What?" No way. But the black granite bubbled at my feet. "Crap. I'm melting it like tar. Am I that hot?"

"You must be, but I can't feel your heat. Can you get your temp down? I can't get to you. Heck, I can't believe this rock can melt."

"Well, it is." It continued to bubble outward, a hot, sticky mess.

"Cool it now. You're right on the edge."

Sheesh. Like I couldn't see that.

"How am I supposed to—" The edge oozed away at my feet. Shoot.

"Silvie!"

I slipped over the side as he yelled.

The ocean rose up, so stony cold.

"*Don't fight the fall,*" Faith growled in my head.

"*You could have told me it was this kind of fall,*" I screamed back.

"*Raise your arms and tuck your head in.*"

"*I'd better survive this. What kind of best friend are you?*"

Damn. Two-hundred feet. It was a death drop, but Faith would never desert me. I kept that at the forefront of my mind as the icy waves loomed.

I hit hard and plunged deep. My breath was knocked out of me.

No.

Not deep. I was in the dark.

Where on earth was I?

I grabbed my sides, patted around to my back. Nothing was wet, and the sensation of 'porting was strong. Oh boy. Had I just 'ported?

"Did I come into another skill, Faith?"

"Yes, so cool. I wish I could have been there."

"So do I, because I really wanna rip your head off for not telling me. You are so gonna get it."

"A 'porter has to move fast to initiate their first speed jump, and yours was complicated by your fire skill's energy burst. This way you're dealing with both at once."

"Don't try and wriggle your way out of this. I just speed-jumped into a black hole. I didn't get a chance to attach a location or coordinates."

"Yeah, but your explosive heat was contained in the hole."

"Guy will be freaking out."

"Then I'll go so you can talk to him. Just make sure you come up with a soft place to land." She closed the link.

Unbelievable. I had to 'port free of this hole and since I was on foreign soil, with no way back to Peacio, the only choice I had was Guy's room. Grrreat. I braced myself as I brought his room's image into my mind. I added the coordinates and let go. Then slammed down.

I crashed into his bed. The wooden legs snapped and collapsed and everything creaked and groaned, including me.

The glare of light coming through his window was punishing, and when I dragged in a breath, it rattled around in my chest and barely made it back out.

"Guy." I threw open our link.

"Where the hell are you? You disappeared into thin air." His voice was panicked, well, beyond panicked.

"Bring a healer, okay. I landed on your bed."

"At the speed you were going? That's where you landed?"

"Calm down. I didn't exactly have a choice."

"I'll grab Nicolas and be there in two seconds."

My belly rolled, and I bit back bile. *"I'm sorry I argued with you."*

"Which argument?"

"All of them." Blood dribbled from my mouth and pooled on his pillow. *"Hurry."*

"I'm almost there." The air stirred, and Guy's guttural groan echoed around the room. He knelt and carefully took my hand. "I'm here. Stay very still. The healer will fix this."

A tall warrior with a whiskered jaw and intense blue eyes bent and peered at me. A light radiated in a gentle glow all around him. "I'm hallucinating. He looks like an angel."

The man laid a hand on my head. "Where does it hurt? The most?"

"You should ask me where it doesn't hurt."

"Gotcha." His hand was warm. No, more than that. His healing-heat increased in strength and blasted out. "I'm Nicolas, one of the leading eight."

"Nice to meet you." I didn't care who he was, as long as he took this pain away.

"Take it easy. Do you not have the skill to fast-heal?"

"No, and I'm kinda wishing I did."

"Silvie." Guy stroked my fingers, his tone a warning.

"It looks worse than it is."

"It looks pretty bad."

"I survived, and see, I'm arguing with you again. That's a good sign."

Nicolas glided his hands down my body. His aura glowed brighter, his touch hotter. "There isn't anything I can't fix. Let me get started."

"What did she break?" Guy tucked my hair behind my ear.

"So far I've got a punctured lung from a broken rib, a ruptured spleen, and some internal bleeding." His wicked heat radiated to all those places, and then traveled down my spine. "She's crushed two of her lower vertebrae, dislocated her hips and—"

"You know, Nicolas," I wriggled my fingers within Guy's as the feeling returned to them. "You'd be more helpful without the commentary."

Nicolas switched his gaze to Guy. "She's your mate?"

"Cousin."

"No, she's not. As I heal, I can feel the mated bond pulsing between you both."

I hiccupped as my damaged lung inflated and tingled anew. "We're mated, but not doing anything about it."

"It's okay if your relationship is new and you're wary." He slid his hands carefully under my lower back, until his fingers rested over my spine. The nerves pinched together, and feeling flooded back.

Guy cleared his throat. "Silvie is a Moyer, and we're distantly related. We just can't go there."

"So, you're truly cousins?" Nicolas looked between Guy and me.

"Far-removed, but yes," Guy answered.

Nicolas ran his hands over my thighs and down my legs. "There's one break and a twisted ankle. I can heal both, but you'll have to take it easy. Your balance will be off."

"I'll rest."

"Good." He smoothed around my calves and continued to work down until he'd encircled my feet. Bones popped and refused. His golden glow slowly diminished. "The healing is complete." He rose to his full towering height. "But take care, as I said. You'll be extremely sore for a few days."

Compassion shone in his eyes.

"Thank you, Nicolas." Now, that was something I never thought I'd say to a warrior.

And now, what did I say to Guy?

Chapter 9

"You're not to move." Guy paced the short space at the end of the room after Nicolas had left. He shoved his tan shirtsleeves up.

"So far I haven't." I rubbed my achy chest. What could I do to calm him?

"How bad is the pain?" He knelt beside me.

"I can handle it, with some bed rest. You couldn't whip to Earth and grab me some pain killers, could you?" Keeping him busy might help.

"I'll do better than that. I'll take you home. You should be with your family, not here amongst strangers."

"You're not a stranger, and I've got the girls' problem to deal with."

"You can deal with that after you've rested. Nicolas said a couple of days." His pale blue gaze swept me from head to toe. "How could I have let this happen?"

"I heard him, but I should still stay." I gripped his hand. "Please stop blaming yourself. This isn't your fault."

"On both those counts we disagree." He scooped me up with the gentlest touch. "You're going home. Enough damage has been done here. Close your eyes."

"Can't we at least talk about this?"

"We've already talked. Close your eyes or I'll blindfold

you."

"You're so obstinate." Still, I squeezed my eyes shut.

"Thank you."

"It wasn't a compliment."

"Keep your eyes shut."

"I am." Only as he 'ported, I couldn't. I needed a way back in. One look. That's all it would take so I had the image.

As we passed through the dome room, I memorized the space. Yuck. It was nothing like I'd imagined, although the smell was the same. So dark and dungeon-like. There weren't even any doors, just four gloomy walls constructed of a gray-black brick with slabs of floor-stones in a dull gray-green. Aged cracks in the floor's surface oozed with slimy green moss, and right there in the center, a well. It was no wonder not one protector had ever visualized this as the entry point. Even I couldn't believe it. Not that I would ever reveal it. No one could know I held the knowledge. I slammed my eyes shut as we continued on.

"Here we are. Your room." Guy's voice rumbled over my head as we arrived.

I lifted my eyelids. "What do we do now?"

He walked to the bed and carefully laid me down. "What we discussed at the cliff. Our memories will sustain us."

"What?" He couldn't mean this was it.

"I had to get you out of Dralion without any argument. I'll speak to Faith and make sure she's aware you're not going back in."

"You can't be serious?" He couldn't leave me. Not now.

"You fell off a cliff, and then broke almost every bone in your body. It's my job to keep you safe, not to see to your harm."

"It wasn't your fault I speed-jumped. I'd have rather it not been off a cliff, but you were there and brought a healer."

"You have your own healers here, and you would have found a softer place to land had you been here." He gripped my hands between his. "And now one of the leading eight is aware I'm mated. No more, Silvie. You're not going back into Dralion."

"You want to end things, just like that?"

"I've aided you as Faith foresaw."

"I still have to get back there. I haven't done what's needed. I haven't even gotten close." What else could I say to convince him?

"Maybe you've done enough, and if you haven't, you'll have to do it from afar."

"You don't want to be a part of this anymore?"

"I can't watch you get hurt again."

"I'm not ready." My chest squeezed in on itself. I couldn't lose him, not now. "I want more time with you."

"As I do with you, but we're getting dangerously close to the point of no return." He pressed my hands to his chest. "I wish you every happiness, and—"

How dare he? I jerked free. "Don't you dare trivialize what's between us by saying you wish me well."

"I'll tell Faith to bring the pain killers." He stepped back, his expression anguished.

"Great. You do that." I squeezed my eyes shut. I couldn't watch him go, not after all we'd been through. He was the one man I should always be able to count on, and now he was going.

"Get plenty of rest."

"Go."

The air moved. My arm hairs bristled, and I slowly opened my eyes.

He was gone.

Tears fell. I gripped his mother's ring and tore it off. I wanted to toss it, to never lay eyes on it again, but instead I shoved it on the third finger of my right hand, where it fit the best.

"Hey."

Faith shut the door behind her and strode to the bed. She popped the lid on a bottle of water and passed me a packet of pills. "I saw. Sorry."

"Don't be sorry, just help me out of these clothes, and no, I don't want to talk about it."

"Water and pills first." She passed them across and I downed them.

"I should have thought of a softer landing, only there wasn't much choice."

"You did just fine, and Nicolas healed you. Wiggle up, okay? But slowly." Gently, she eased the leather pants down my legs, and then with as much care as she could, unbuttoned my shirt and slipped it off my arms.

"My pajamas are in the dresser."

"Gotcha." She found a brushed cotton top with yellow sunflowers embroidered on the pockets, and white pajama shorts. My favorite set. "Are you sure you don't want to talk?"

"Absolutely." I changed and eased my head onto my pillow. "I can't believe he's gone."

"You had next to nowhere to land, and he feels responsible for your injuries." She scooted onto the golden covers beside me and pulled her knees to her chest. "He just needs some time."

"Do you think Nicolas will be a problem? He knew we were mated, but we told him we were cousins."

"Physically and emotionally it goes against the grain for healers to bring any harm to another. Think of Belle. She's compassionate, kind and understanding. Healers, and those with empathy, have the same qualities."

"Well, Guy's gone." And my heart was lodged like a stone in my chest. "Have you had any further forewarning?"

"No. Perhaps he's done all he needed to in assisting you. You've always been the key, not him."

I turned onto my side and winced. "I hate that I miss him."

Soothingly, she rubbed my arm. "I'm always with you."

I yawned. "I'm so tired, and sore."

"Then get some rest. I'll watch over you."

"We stick together," I mumbled as I tried to keep my eyes open, only the dark took me.

Sleep. I so needed sleep.

* * * *

"Silvie?"

Faith's voice rattled around in my head.

"Yeah?"

"Just checking on you." She'd been with me for the past two days, but this morning I'd sent her to school.

"I've showered, eaten, and now I'm back in bed. Are you taking notes for me?"

"Yep. What do your bruises look like today?"

I lifted my shirt and touched the dark marks across my chest, most of them in line with the injuries I'd sustained. *"A touch better than yesterday."*

"Then get some more sleep."

It was lunchtime, and Friday. At least I had the weekend ahead. I plumped my pillow and snuggled deeper. I dreamed of Guy, of his soft lips brushing across my forehead, only my dream flittered away before I could grab hold of him.

The dark ensued.

* * * *

Hot.

Why did it feel so hot?

I lifted my heavy eyelids and blinked against the bright midday sunshine streaming into the room. Faith tied the golden folds of velvet back. "Did you have to open those?"

"That's not like you. You love the sunshine."

"Because I don't feel like me. The one man I should be able to count on ditched me, and I have to soldier on. Again. My life sucks, and I still have to fix your problem."

"Don't worry about my problem right now. You need to

heal first. You'll feel more like yourself once you get moving, and it's time." She tugged her blond ponytail as she crossed to me. "And before Saturday's completely gone."

I wriggled my toes. The aches were gone, the bruising having mellowed more to a splotchy yellow.

"Oh, and check out the flower someone brought you."

In a fluted glass vase, a single golden rose with a deep red center bloomed. Next to it was a note. I picked it up. Please let this rose be from—no. Soldier on.

Dear Silvie,

Vitaria says hello. She asked about you. I told her of your accident, that you're not coming back. This rose is from her, and I asked Hope to pass it along.

You'd better be taking care of yourself.
Guy.

Well, no words of I miss you there. My heart had certainly taken a beating, just like my body had.

"The flower's from Vitaria. Hope dropped it and Guy's note off." I passed her the sheet of crisp paper.

"I've met Vitaria. It's so sad about her mother's illness." She frowned as she read. "Hope hasn't dropped by today. Silas and Davio snuck in while you slept this morning, but not Hope."

"You must have missed her." I eased my legs over the side of the bed. "Okay, I agree. It's time to get moving."

"And what are we going to do now we're moving?" She held me steady, helping me find my feet.

"Not we, me. I want to cook, and no, you don't have to help." My kitchen was the only place I longed to be, and right now I needed some space for what I had in mind. I was about to prepare Guy and his father a meal. I had to get closure, and cooking was the only way.

I showered, and then changed into a pair of hip-hugging

jeans and my favorite flame-red t-shirt. Okay, time to 'port, and to get it right this time. I brought the image of my kitchen into my mind, and from one second to the next, I was there. Oh yeah, so cool. At least for a moment, my heart lightened. I tapped the bright red countertop, and a small sense of peace stole through me. It would be enough to keep me going, or it better be.

Time for that meal. I opened the fridge. The shelves were stocked, and I took out a cut of beef, one the perfect size for a small roast.

I mixed it with herbs, set it into a deep dish then slid it into the oven to cook. Next, I prepped the vegetables, peeling sweet potatoes and pumpkin. I scattered them over another oven pan and popped it in too.

While the roast cooked, I foraged in my garden. Mmm, fresh beans and mint. Those would be perfect. I sliced and steamed them. With the meat done, I skimmed off the juices and made a rich gravy, one bursting with all the right flavors.

I plated two dishes then opened my link to Silas. *"Hey, Faith said you dropped by."*

"Yeah, but you clearly needed the rest so I didn't wake you. Do you feel better now?"

"A bit. I'm in my kitchen and I—"

He shimmered into the room, sword dangling from his hand and his loose white shirt plastered to his sweaty skin. Davio blinked in beside him, heaving in deep breaths, his black jeans sticking as damply to him. Silas pulled me into a hug. "I hated seeing you down like that."

"Yuck, you're all wet." I pushed him away. "Training?"

"Yep, just finished a session. That looks suspiciously like dinner." Silas sheathed his sword. "You shouldn't have done that. You should be taking it easy."

"I made this meal for Guy and his father, as a final farewell. They'll be eating separately, but I need permission to take this second plate to the cells."

Davio squeezed my shoulder. "Of course you have permission. You've been there before. I'll let the guards know you're on your way."

"Thanks."

After another wet hug from each of them, they flashed away.

I'd take Guy his meal first. Plates in hand, I brought the image of the stables into my mind. I made the jump, jolted down with a little wobble. Not bad. I'd get better.

I searched the interior, but all was clear. The scents of hay and dust permeated the air. The last time I'd been in here, Guy had kissed me. It had been right after my training session with Zayn on the beach. Boy, I shouldn't think about Guy's kisses. It wasn't like—yeah, I shouldn't think about them at all. Hopefully this heartache would lesson with time, or it better. I crossed to Guy's workbench and set one of the foiled plates down next to an opened notebook. Guy's. It was filled with an almost illegible scrawl. Spells probably.

"Hey, Silvie."

Hope strode into the room, slapping her Stetson against her leg.

"Hey."

"I didn't know you were up. I was coming by tonight." She squeezed me, nice and gentle.

"Thanks for visiting me while I was sick. I got the rose you dropped off from Vitaria. Well, that Guy had you drop off."

"What rose?"

Hmm, maybe I hadn't dreamt of Guy being there and kissing me in my sleep. Maybe he had dropped it off. Oh well, it didn't matter if he had. It changed nothing. "Ah, never mind."

"If you're sure." She eyed the covered plate, and then me with a smile. "Mm-mmm, is that a roast I smell?"

"Yes, but for Guy. Could you tell him it's here? Let him know this is my way of leaving one last memory. Tell him to enjoy the meal, just as his father soon will." I backed away, one of the dishes still in hand.

"Hold on. What do you mean just as his father soon—"

I 'ported before she could question me further. Best to get out of there, anyway.

Within the bleakness of the cells, I arrived. The first pull of air into my lungs was so rotten my stomach heaved. A single lantern on the wall cast a small glow over the passageway of gray bricks. Warrick stood on guard ahead, one of the protectors from within Davio's inner circle. He was a giant of a man, his black hair plastered wetly to his scalp from the heat inside the dank chambers. The heat was good. I didn't mind it at all.

I walked toward him, and he swung to look at me. "Davio said you were on your way."

"I've brought a meal for Gerritt Moyer."

"At least he's one of the more civil prisoners we have. I'll take you through." He led the way down a stairwell and deeper into the lower recesses.

"Silvie?"

Guy's voice rebounded inside my head and I stumbled to a stop. I'd not expected to hear from him, not like this. *"Is it really you?"*

"I'm staring at—are you seriously giving my father the same?"

"That's what I told Hope. I'm on my way to him now." I slogged on.

"One last memory? Thank you." His words sounded rough, as if he struggled to hold back his emotions.

We stopped outside a cell completely enclosed within steel. Such absolute construction was the only way we could contain our enemy, to prevent them from 'porting, 'pathing and anything else in between. *"I'm going to lose this connection with you when I join him. Do you have any words you want me to pass along?"*

"Yes, tell him you're my mate, and that he's not to harm you. Show him the ring otherwise he might. Tell him I love him, and that I'll see him freed. Tell him—"

"Okay, I think I get it."

"I want to hear how he is."

"You ready?" Warrick eyed me as he slid the key into the lock then removed a set of handcuffs from his side belt.

"Yes." To Guy, I said, *"I wish we could keep chatting, but I've gotta go."*

"Just show him the ring."

Warrick turned the key, and with a loud snick it unlocked. He pushed the door open and disappeared within.

"Did you hear me, Silvie? Show him the ring."

"I heard. I will, but he can't hurt me."

"We're enchanters, so don't look into his eyes until he's seen the ring."

"Okay, I get it. Relax." He couldn't help himself. He'd always want to see to my care, not that the opportunity would arise anymore.

Low tones came from within then Warrick returned. "We keep then underfed, so he's weak, but I've still restrained him for your protection. Keep your eyes averted from his at all times. Knock on the door once you're done."

"Okay." My heart thumped as Warrick passed me a lantern. I stepped into the cell, and Warrick closed the heavy metal door with a clunk.

I lifted my lantern, adding its glow to the barely lit candle flickering on the floor. I edged forward, my gaze moving over the man propped against the top rail of a metal pallet. A ratty gray blanket covered his legs, and his arms were outstretched, each of his thin wrists restrained with cuffs and pulled back against hooks.

His face was gaunt, his coal-black hair long and shaggy, and his eyes—

I ducked my head, but not before I'd seen they were the same shade as Guy's with that beautiful rim of silver. "You look just like him," I murmured.

"Like who?" His voice was raspy, deeper than Guy's and full of cynicism.

"Your son." I should have expected the likeness since we didn't physically age.

"Guy better look a lot healthier than me. How do you know my son?"

"I'm Silvie." I shuffled closer. "Guy and I are soul-bound, although since I'm a Peacian, it didn't work out."

He let out a snort of breath. "Unbelievable. You're truly his mate?"

"Yes. I brought you a meal, that's if you'll accept it."

"We don't get fed any more than the scraps in here. Of course I'll accept it. Come closer."

I crossed and sat as close as needed.

"Is that"—he jerked on his iron bindings—"my wife's ring? You spoke the truth?"

From my finger, it glinted in the candlelight.

"Yes." I removed the plate's foil covering. "Guy said to tell you not to harm me, to show you the ring as proof." I picked up the knife and fork I'd set beside the slab of beef and cut a small slice of meat.

"I can't harm anyone trussed up like this." He jiggled his legs under the blanket and his chains scraped together.

"Take this slowly, okay?" I slid the fork between his opened lips. Oh my, his eyes were so piercing, like Guy's. I missed looking into Guy's eyes.

"You don't appear afraid of me." His stomach rumbled as he ate.

"Honestly? I haven't seen Guy for a bit, and it's kind of nice seeing you. The similarities and all. I made the same meal for Guy. He wants to know how you are."

"Hungry for more." He jerked his head toward the plate. "Please."

I speared a cube of roasted potato and pumpkin and fed it to him next.

He chewed, mumbling around his mouthful. "He would love this. It tastes just like the roasts his mother used to make."

I cut another piece of beef and swirled it through the gravy then popped it into his mouth. "He misses her, and you, badly."

"You sound as if you've gotten to know him."

"I have. He has a heart of gold. I'll miss him."

"Tell him I love him. That the moment these buffoons slip up, even once, I'll come to him."

"Buffoons?" I fed him some of the beans.

"Hey, not the greens, the meat. I need to build my strength."

I forked even more of the beans and slipped it between his lips. "Take back the buffoons comment and I will."

He let out a spurt of laughter, one which caught him by surprise by the look in his eyes. "Sure, but I'll only take it back if you promise me the meat."

"I promise."

"Lots of gravy too." He licked his lips. "And they're not buffoons. They're angels, and always granting me my every wish."

I laughed. "Angels? You really must want the meat." I cut a large slab and fed him.

He half finished his mouthful before he mumbled his response. "Enchanters are wise, clever and very sneaky. Have you not learned that from Guy yet?"

"I agree to the wise and clever, but sneaky?" I continued feeding him, until not a smear of food remained on the plate.

"Guy's mother and I could never keep him pinned to one place. As a child, he was as mischievous as ten children put together."

Oh, I could listen to tales about Guy all day. "I'm glad to

have met him, and you, no matter the circumstances. I want to come again, although, I need to ask a favor. I want you to accept something else from me."

"That depends."

"Guy won't take his mother's ring back, but it's not truly mine. I don't think I can move on while I'm still holding onto it. And, well, you're the only person I can safely give this to, in the hope that one day it'll get back to him. It should stay with your family." I slid the ring from my finger. "Guy said to say he loved you too, and that he would see you freed, although don't count on that last part, not considering where you are."

"I can't take the ring." A tear formed in the corner of his eye. "As much as I long to."

"Why not?"

"Silvie who? What last name did Guy give you?"

"How did you—"

"It was foretold, by his mother. Did Guy give you his last name?"

"Um, yeah, but only under duress. I don't hold it anymore."

He pulled on his shackles, jarring them against his wrists. "Put the ring back on. It's enchanted, Silvie. Before his mother gave it to him she had me cast a spell over it, one which would ensure it would find its way to the woman he would name as his. The spell would draw you together. She had the all-seeing eye, and the spell she had me create was strong. It was bound by the endless circle of love within it."

Crap. "Are you serious?"

"I'll never forget the spell. Where love and destiny meet, where two hearts beat, so shall the giver adore. Where sacrifice is made, where fire and magic are laid, only one shall be restored. Her name shall be Moyer, with golden fingers and a heart so pure. Her man will bow down, and shall never go hungry before her." He grabbed in a deep breath. "His mother said you're the key. You must always hold the ring, now he's named you as his."

"Why would she—" Crap. Crap. Crap. The whole universe was aligning against me. I still had Faith's problem to fix, and now I had a spelled ring I couldn't give— "Hold on. How do you know I have the fire skill, the golden fingers? What did your wife mean by 'I'm the key?'" Faith's words rebounded in my head, her insistence I was the key. Yeah, I'd really heard enough of that lately.

"I've always kept my wife's skill quiet. Although, somewhere in her history, one of her ancestors had to have been fathered by a Wincrest. The skill only runs through the two ruling families of Magio. Anyway, before her death, she spoke of a forewarning, and she had me enchant the ring to ensure Guy's destiny was set on the right path. He doesn't know about the spell. He never needed to, not since she didn't wish any further interference than what was cast."

"Holy moly." No wonder Guy and I had met even though he'd tried to steer clear of me. Our destiny had been set all right. "This is crazy." Yet it made more sense than I liked.

"Wear the ring. The magic within it is strong."

I shoved the ring back on.

"Not your right hand, your left." His jerked his head toward it. "The other hand. Now. The magic will be stronger still if you accept your destiny is with Guy."

"You know, I can see where Guy gets his stubbornness from. Truly, he won't want this, and how on earth can you want your son's destiny to be with me? We're enemies you and I."

"My son's happiness will always come first, and his mother was never wrong. Because of the war and the dome my father enchanted over Dralion, so few of our people are finding their mated one. Our skills continue within our family lines, but they don't return to full strength unless we're born of the mated bond. How many centuries has it been since the fire skill was seen? And why must Guy be one of the few left to enchant? We are losing the battle, and it is with ourselves more than any other."

My heart ached at the truth in his words. "Are there other warriors like you who believe the same?"

"A handful, but the number grows."

"Are you loyal to Wincrest?"

"Yes, do not mistake my words. He is a wise ruler, and my allegiance is to him and Dralion."

"Okay, so tell me how I'm the key?" Because that would really be helpful.

"My wife told me my son's mate would hold the greatest of the battle skills, and yet you brought me food, your enemy. You have the heart of a nurturer, as she did. Never forget the fullness of the spell." Again he jerked his head toward the ring. "Swap it to the third finger of your left hand. Within your heart, bind yourself to Guy."

"Guy is going to fight any such binding. We've already released each other." Yet still, with shaky fingers, I swapped it to my other hand and pushed it over my knuckle and into place. My heart thundered within my chest as the truth blazed back at me. "I'm falling for him. I made this meal to give myself closure, but deep down, I did it to reconnect with him. To bring him back to me."

"A part of his soul lives within you, Silvie. Why wouldn't you want to have him close? Embrace the bond. Allow the magic to flow."

"I want to be with him." I traced the ring with my finger. Slowly it heated, as if the magic within bubbled to life. As if the ring were in its rightful place. "I will be with him." I stated the words forcefully. "I will be with him." The ring lit to a bright golden hue.

"That's perfect. That light proves the magic beats strong. The light will cool and disperse soon." A smile lifted his lips. "Never let my son walk away from you again."

"I won't." The light slowly faded from the ring.

Peacefulness settled over me. Even though I didn't have Guy back, I wouldn't give up. I never should have.

The key jingled in the lock and the door was jarred open. Warrick walked in, observing all with his gaze. "You've been a while, and I thought I'd check. Are you done, Silvie?"

"Yes."

I nodded at Gerritt and offered a small smile. "Until the next time we meet."

"Thank you for the meal. It's the best I've had in a very long time."

I walked out. My mate's father needed to be freed, only I could never be the one to do it. I could not lay down my loyalty to Carlisio Loveria or Davio, and freeing one of Dralion's warriors who had raised arms in battle against one of my own would be seen as exactly that.

What a tangled weave, yet I was another step closer to what I needed. I was the key. Faith, and now Guy's mother had both decreed it so, one from this time, and one through a spell enchanted so many years ago. Which meant, I had some serious work ahead of me.

In the darkened depths of the passageway, I eyed the long row of steel doors. So many captured warriors, and did any of them hold the beliefs that Guy's father did? That we were losing the battle, and with ourselves and no other. We were one world, yet with two nations at war.

"*Guy.*" I threw open our link now I was clear of the steel cell preventing it. "*I need to see you.*"

"*I'm waiting for an update. I'm already in your room.*"

The update. Oh, he was definitely going to get an update. My heart raced as I 'ported to my room. He leaned against the far wall. His jaw was rough with stubble, his eyes darkened with circles. "You don't look so good."

"I've been helping with the station's muster. Long nights and even longer days." He slapped a black Stetson against his leg. His white shirttails hung crinkled and loose over his jeans, the buttons askew, done up with one out of order. "How is he?"

"Ah, strong of mind. Determined. He loves you, Guy."

And I had to be as equally determined as his father if I wanted my mate back. Sneaky too. Yeah, and I had the perfect idea to set things in motion.

I crossed to my dressing room and rummaged through the racks. Yes, the perfect dress. I pulled out a short, slinky red number and a pair of four-inch matching red heels.

"Is that all you're going to tell me?" His gaze drilled into me from the doorway. "What are you doing?"

"There's more, but it's Saturday night, and I'd like to go out." I circled my fingers in the air. "Turn around, please."

As I lifted the hem of my shirt, he spun about. "Wait, you can't get changed in front of me."

"Well, you're the one standing in my dressing room doorway. Your father enjoyed the meal by the way."

"What does he look like? And you're going out where?"

"Dancing, and he needs more food. I'll make sure he gets some more on a regular basis." I slipped the dress over my head. It fit snugly around my waist, skimmed my hips and clung to my thighs.

"The dancing. You didn't say where."

"Where most people dance. A nightclub. Have you ever been to one of those on Earth?" I flicked my hair over my shoulder as I sashayed past him. "Where's my purse? Ah, there it is."

"No, there's never been time."

"Do you have time now?" I pulled out my favorite lippy, dabbed it on then dropped it in my purse.

"I have work."

"At this time of the night?"

"I told you we're mustering." He plunked his hat on. "The station never sleeps."

"Come out with me instead. Let loose and have some fun."

"I can't."

"Then I'll just have to find someone else who I can have fun with." I winked, and without a moment's hesitation, flashed away.

Chapter 10

"Please follow. Please follow." Fingers crossed, I arrived in a side alley on Tauranga's waterfront strand. Above me the sky was a dark ribbon of black, twinkling with a heavenly array of stars. Music pulsed through the air from nearby clubs. The perfect night for seduction.

That's if he came. I needed him to come.

The air swirled and he shimmered into view. Tingles raced across my skin.

"Damn it, Silvie. You did that on purpose."

"That's because I prefer your company over anyone else's." I ducked past him and out onto the sidewalk.

Okay, so I'd gotten him here, now it was time to throw him completely out of his element. His father thought Guy was sneaky, but I had every intention of outdoing him.

He clomped after me across the cobbles. "I shouldn't be here."

Giving my hips an extra swing, I grinned at him over my shoulder. "With the way you're dressed, you'll fit right in at the Bulldog Saloon."

"What I'm going to do is take you home. It's late, and you've only just recovered from your injuries. You shouldn't be out dancing."

No sirreee. He was not taking me home. I picked up my

pace and dashed through the entranceway of the western styled club. He wouldn't be able to 'port me out of here. People simply couldn't disappear before one's eyes on this world.

"Silvie, wait."

I scurried toward the bar.

"What'll it be, miss?" The shirtless bartender hooked one thumb into his dark jeans. His studded, black leather vest swung loose.

"Nothing," Guy answered as he came up on my rear.

"I'll take two Cokes, thanks."

"What's a Coke?" Guy growled in my ear.

"Something to wet your throat." Sliding back, I rested against him.

"Here you go, miss."

I paid the bartender and passed Guy a drink. "To the mated bond."

"Just one drink. Then we're out of here."

"And a dance."

He tossed back his drink.

Taking my time, I sipped and tapped my foot to the music. As the thumping beat finally mellowed to a softer number, I set my glass down. "Okay, this is the perfect song."

"I'm sure it is." He did not look happy.

"Dance with me? Please." I twined my arms around his neck and nudged him onto the floor. "It'll give me a chance to tell you what else your father said."

"All right, but make it quick." His scowl died away as he tucked me closer. "Very quick."

"He said you were as mischievous as ten children put together, that you were difficult to keep pinned down as a child. I don't think you've changed." I pushed onto my toes and pressed a kiss to his cheek. He was the one I wanted. Him, and only him.

"Is there anything else?"

"He said your mother's ring is enchanted. Before she gave

it to you, she had him cast a spell over it, one which would ensure it would find its way to the woman you would name as yours. The spell she had him create was strong. He said it was bound by the endless circle of love within it."

"Damn it." He gripped my waist. "My mother seriously had him enchant her ring?"

"Yes. He told me the spell."

"Speak it." His pale blue eyes blazed.

"Where love and destiny meet, where two hearts beat, so shall the giver adore. Where sacrifice is made, where fire and magic are laid, only one shall be restored. Her name shall be Moyer, with golden fingers and a heart so pure. Her man will bow down, and shall never go hungry before her."

"Hell." His chest rattled as he sucked in a long breath. "That's one potent spell."

"Your mother also said I was the key, and we both know who else we've heard that from."

"My mother wanted us together?"

"Yes, and so do I, but do you?"

"I never wanted to leave you." He steered me toward a darkened, secluded corner, pressed me against the wall. Trapped. Not that I minded.

"You still look angry."

Hands planted on the wall each side of my head, he leaned in. "I've hated our parting. I can't sleep, and the only food I've managed to eat these past three days is the roast you made me. All I see are your blue eyes when I close mine at night. I want you, but I still don't see how this can work."

"Neither do I, but I can't watch you walk away again. When I was with your father, he helped me to see things clearer. He told me to wear the ring on my left hand, to accept my destiny and to bind myself to you."

He seized my hand. "That's what you did?"

"With my heart and soul."

"Damn it." His gaze was agonized. "I can't keep denying what's between us. I don't want to live without you either." The silver flared to life in his eyes. "For the girl whose heart is aligned with mine, may it always keep in perfect time. May her fighting spirit never fail, and from now and until the end of our days…may she be the woman I forever praise."

"Oh." What a beautiful spell. "Did you truly mean—"

"Go out with me and agree to a date. I promise right now, I'll never be late."

"Ah—"

"Once I start rhyming, it's hard to stop. Once my muse is lit, it's one that shines bright. If you ever wish me to slow or even to—"

I kissed him, and he grinned against my lips and kissed me back.

"I take back my words of release, Silvie. You're mine and no one else's."

"And if you ever touch another woman, I'll singe her."

Hands cupping my face, he murmured, "We stick together, now and forever."

"Deal, and I'm very good at brokering those."

"Then I'm brokering another." He tucked a lock of my hair behind my ear. "You've only just recovered from your injuries, and I'm exhausted. It's time for bed."

"Well, since you asked so nicely. My bed. Let's go." I had no problem with this request.

We snuck out and into the closest darkened alley. In a flash, we returned. Yay. Home.

I kicked off my heels and slung my purse onto my nightstand. "My room is your room."

"Great." Rolling into bed, he tipped me in with him. "My mate is my mate."

I stroked his stubbly jaw, looking deep into his stunning eyes. "Are we really together?"

"You need more confirmation?"

"It would help." This was real, but our words of release had been too. "Could you—I mean, could we un-release each other properly?"

"Yes. I should have suggested it. I'll start." His voice turned husky, as if he fought his emotions. "Silvie, you hold the other half of my soul and I, yours. I wish to be bound to you, to keep you safe and to cherish you, to give you all you desire, and…to never let you go again. It's been a living hell without you." He kissed me, deep and slowly.

Wow. I was strong, but I needed him. My enchanter. No wonder Faith and Hope had worked so hard to make their relationships work. It made total sense now, no matter the future difficulties we faced. We'd deal with it all, together.

"My turn." I couldn't wait to speak my words. "Guy, my heart and soul are bound to yours. I wish to give you all you desire, for us to work together side by side. I wish to cherish you, to keep you close, and to pester you for all time to come."

"Pester?" He nipped my butt. "Yep, you already have that well under control."

Happiness swelled in my heart and bubbled over. "Trust me, I can pester with the best of them. You haven't seen the half of it yet."

Eyes twinkling, he rolled over top of me. "Then show me the other half."

"Oh, you've got it. Pestering coming up." Heat flared through my body. Fire flickered on my fingertips, although with one thought I snuffed it out. "Okay, just don't get me too hot."

"I like hot."

So did I. I caught his face and dragged his mouth to mine. I got bossy, until the air surely pulsed with my heat. Perfect. I had my mate back and my soul at peace. Nothing more could surpass this moment.

* * * *

I wriggled and rubbed my feet against Guy's jean clad legs. He still slept like the dead even though it was mid-afternoon. Lucky for him, I didn't care to get up either, no matter I was wide awake.

"I'm tired," he mumbled under his breath as he stirred.

"Go back to sleep. I'm not going anywhere." I brought fire to my fingertips and bounced the tiny flames in short spurts.

"Mmm, closer." Throwing one leg over mine, he all but smothered me. "Why can I smell—" He cranked one eye open. "Ahh, didn't your parents teach you not to play with fire?"

"Nope." I blew on the tips and the flames flickered brighter. Oooh, so pretty.

He wet his thumb and finger then pinched one of the tips and extinguished it.

"There're nine more still to go."

"Put them all out before you burn something."

I relit the one he'd snuffed. "I've got this under control."

"So do I." He wrapped his hands around mine.

"Hey." With no choice, I doused the flames in one go. "You are no fun right now."

"We should talk some more, since we're awake. Faith and Hope's problem bugged me the entire time we were apart."

"That's because all roads still lead to Dralion, and you know I'm going back there."

"I've already said no to Dralion."

"Yeah, but that's where their issue exists. I can't fix it from here."

"I'm not taking you to Dralion."

"You don't have a choice. Wincrest wants you to continue the Moyer line, and eventually he's going to meet me."

He frowned. "Damn, in my happiness, that slipped my mind. Still, you're not going to Dralion. You have culinary school next year, and your education is important."

"Peacio is my home, but so is being with you. Your fellow

warriors will surely begin to notice your longer periods of time away."

"I'm in the outback half the time. I'll just explain it that way." With the back of his fingers, he stroked my cheek. "Your safety remains imperative."

"I'm safe when I'm with you, and I can handle spending a little time in Dralion as needed."

"It's not needed."

"Yes, it is. I'm going."

"No, you're not."

"You're being difficult."

"I'm being reasonable."

"We have to work together on sorting the girls' problem, and we need to get it fixed now. Give me a second to get ready." I eased out of his hold and bounded into my dressing room. Fishing around, I found dark leather pants and a fitted black t-shirt, the closest I had to warrior attire.

After changing, I marched back to the bedroom. Guy hadn't moved other than to cross his arms behind his head.

"Will you take me?" I ran my thumb over his forehead, smoothing out the deep worry lines.

"No."

"I can't let Faith or Hope down, because if either is forced to marry another, I can assure you, Davio and Silas won't rest until they get their mates back. You think we're at war now, but it will be far greater if those men lose their soul-bound ones to slayers."

"They won't lose them."

"No, that's right. They won't." With the image of the dome room at the forefront of my mind, I 'ported.

The floor stones were slick under my feet, and I made the jump straight on to Faith's bedroom. Hopefully, she'd "see" my arrival, because right now, I needed her support. Drat. Her bed was made and her room tidied. She wasn't here.

Guy shimmered into view, his growl fierce as he stormed toward me. "You looked when I last 'ported you."

"I'll never tell, not a single soul. I may despise Wincrest, but I'd never use that hate against you. I'm bound by our bond to keep you safe, just as you are with me. I'd never encourage a war."

"This is too dangerous." He crushed me against him.

"Not if those from Dralion still believe me a warrior. We'll simply tell them I'm your mate as we did with the healer Nicolas. Allow me to have a presence here when needed. Think about it. It'll solve your problem with Wincrest making demands on you, if he believes we're together."

"She's right, Guy." Faith peeked out from her bathroom, cheeks flushed. "You've really got to learn not to argue with Silvie. You'll rarely win a fight."

Hope nudged her chin over Faith's shoulder. "Silvie's loyal to all three of us, and when she's here or at Wincrest Station, she can be a Moyer. Warriors will see her when she's with you, and this is the only way around the problem."

"I can't believe this." Guy raked a hand through his hair. "You two are ganging up on me too."

"You have to agree." I rubbed his chest. "We'll make this work."

"I hate this." He heaved in a deep breath. "But I don't see I have a choice, although I'll only agree on one condition. You never come to Dralion without me, even though you have the image of the dome room. That goes the same for the station. You have to 'path me first to let me know you want to come so I can pick you up. When we travel through the dome room, we're together. When you visit the station, we're together."

"Ah, I get it. Your condition is that we're together." I tapped his nose. "That works for me, big fella."

"Big fella?" He grabbed my finger and kissed the tip. "I'm so angry with you right now. You're too sneaky for your own good."

Faith grinned at Hope. "Aww, don't they make the cutest couple, sis?"

"Yep, and I can't believe our enchanter is settling down. Donaldo will be pleased."

"Talking about Donaldo." Guy paced to the window and shoved the snowy-white curtains aside. "He organized today's games. I haven't forgotten the warriors are gathering in the field. The fire's already lit."

"Did you say a fire?" I edged in under his arm. Oooh, orange and red flames flickered from a massive bonfire in the meadow beyond the gates. "Oh, we so have to go. What kind of games?"

Faith joined us. "Any game involving a weapon, or the skill in using one. The spear, mallet, blade, bow and arrow. They even compete in horse riding."

"Ah, then similar to the games we have in Peacio."

"They're so much fun to watch." Hope nabbed a leather jacket from the end of Faith's bed. "There's food first. We cook meat over the open fire. Some of the warriors even play a few tunes if there's time."

"You said Wincrest organized it?" I tugged on Guy's shirtsleeve.

"Yes, but he only comes once the action is underway."

"So, what are we waiting for? Do I need to remind you there's a fire?"

"No, you don't, and neither will you leave my side." He wrapped an arm around my waist, his grip firm over my hip as he 'ported us.

When we arrived, he bent his head and kissed me. His lips moved over mine with stealth and precision. Loud hoots sounded.

"Ignore them," he murmured against my lips. "I'm trying to prove a point."

"Oh, prove away."

"Okay, enough of that." Faith shoved between us. "The fire's hot, but there's also some heat now coming off you, Silvie. You two have to watch yourselves."

Fire. That's right. I gawked at the flames which burned and sent out a wash of warmth. Two warrior women sat on fallen logs before it, and music floated into the air from flutes they played. Nice. A couple of men strummed guitars in readiness to join them, and many others chattered in groups with drinks in hand. They all appeared so normal. Warriors taking time to relax.

"Are you hungry? We always eat first." Guy closed the gap, stroked with a finger under my chin and brought my gaze back to him. "People are not always as they seem. You'll give them a chance, won't you?"

"Of course she will." Faith played with the top button of her violet shirt. "Or she better. Wait here while I get you both some food." She and Hope walked off toward a trestle table which bulged with an array of food and plated meats.

"Silvie!"

My name was an excited squeal, and as I turned, Vitaria plowed into me. Her blond bob fluttered across my cheeks.

"I've been so worried about you since Guy told me of your nasty speed-jump, but you can 'port. That's so cool."

I hugged her back since it seemed only right. "Nicolas healed me and I rested well. Thank you for the flower."

"The rose was from my mother's garden. I picked one for her and you." She eyed Guy. "Where have you been?"

"With my mate."

She frowned. "Your mate?" Then she smiled, wide. "You've found her?"

Guy tugged me in front of him, his chest against my back. "We had a few issues to work through, but now we're sharing the news."

"Wow." Her eyes lit as brightly as her smile. "That's wonderful. Congrats."

"Did I hear you right?" Nicolas strode in and clapped Guy on the shoulder. "You've finally come to your senses. There's no further secrecy?"

"You heard right." Guy shook his hand. "Thanks for all you did."

"No problem." Nicolas slanted his head toward me. "You're fully healed?"

"Yes. I rested as you said."

"Good, then this is a day for extra celebration. I'll catch you both later. I've promised to play one of the guitars for a bit." Continuing on in his dark leathers, he joined those nearer the fire.

"Oh, there's Hope." Vitaria grinned. "She's a hard one to catch, and I need to ask her if I can come out to the station. I'd love to see the outback. Later, you guys." She raced off.

"I can't believe I'm going to say this, but it feels weird that I'm getting along with—"

"Shh." Guy pressed a finger against my lips as two warriors ambled past, the swords at their sides glinting orange from the firelight. "You truly can't say it."

The strangest emotion rolled through me. It was one of unease, but not for these warriors. All my life I'd been told to hate the enemy. Even Guy's father was imprisoned for bringing harm to my people, but I still liked him. Nicolas and Vitaria too. It was crazy to have these conflicting feelings, but all was not as it seemed. Not every warrior was bad.

Silas had joined with Hope. Davio had accepted Faith. I was no different to my brother and cousin. We'd all found the good in warriors. Faith and Hope also wanted to bring about peace between our nations. Now, I wanted that peace too, so future generations wouldn't have to suffer the loss of their mate as I might have, as Zayn right now did, and who knew who else was in the same boat.

"Hey, you look deep in thought." Guy stroked my nape, his fingers warm and firm around my neck.

"I've had a revelation." I wrapped my arms around his waist and snuggled.

"And that is?"

"We have a huge job ahead of us."

"We already know that."

"It's more than what we spoke of." Heat surged through my veins. "I feel driven, as the girls do."

"Silvie." Faith jogged toward me, grabbed my hand. "Forewarning."

"Not again. Who and how bad?"

"You. Guy, let's go."

He grabbed me and followed Faith's 'porting airstream.

In a blink, I teetered on the edge of an indoor pool. Three lanes wide and seventy or eighty feet long, all surrounded by blue tiled walls. Okay, not good. I did not feel up to a dip.

"Throw her in!" Faith screamed.

Guy tossed me into the depths and the water closed over my head.

Yuck. I shivered at the bottom of the pool, hating the cold. I pushed upward and broke the surface. Water bubbled and steam rose as I shoved my hair out of my face. "Okay, I would like to point out that cold water sucks."

"It's not cold now." Faith eased out from behind a tall stone column, wiped her brow. "It's like a sauna in here. That was one hot blast, and with next to no warning."

Arm outstretched, Guy leaned toward me. "Come here, my little pest."

I swam and grabbed his hand. He lifted me out and into his arms. Water sluiced to my feet.

"Your skill is gaining in intensity." He threaded his fingers through mine. "Sometimes you can control it, and other times you can't. That was certainly one fast flare you had no power over. Your rising must be close."

When one's rising began, an overpowering assault wreaked havoc on all our senses. Adrenaline pumped through our bodies causing an all-time high. Hormones swung, and strength-levels three-times greater than normal hit us. I wasn't ready for that. I hadn't trained enough. Oh boy, during our rising our power was phenomenal. It was certainly an occasion we honored, celebrated and shared with our closest, but my skill was too unpredictable. "I don't have a good enough handle on it yet."

"I know." Faith came closer. "You've cooled again, but if your rising is near, then we need to get you out of Dralion and back home where we don't have to worry about who sees what you can do. It's gotta be close."

"No, you're wrong. My rising could still be days away. My flares might look worse because I have the fire skill. I simply need to train."

"Or it could take hours. What if I'm right? You know the drill."

"Know what drill, Faith?" A man's booming voice traveled to us as he walked through the side doors. "Hell, it's hot in here."

Who was he? Wearing an impeccable red shirt with silver chains looped from his shoulder to his top pocket and long legs encased in tough black leather pants, he appeared a leader of men.

"Ah, there's my granddaughter." He gripped Faith in a firm forearm embrace. Gold insignia rings on his thumbs glinted under the overhead lights. "You and Hope are difficult to find, and none of the staff ever seem to know where either of you are."

Oh boy. This had to be Donaldo Wincrest.

"Hope's out enjoying the games." She turned and acknowledged Guy. "So was I, until Guy insisted he knew of a spell to heat cold water, so I dared him to, um, heat the pool."

Her gaze locked with mine and she opened our connection. *"I have no idea why I didn't get any forewarning he was about to walk in here. Play it cool, okay?"*

"Cool? Are you sure I can't use a little heat on him?"

"He's my grandfather, so no. The blood-bond pulses strongly between the Wincrests. I can't harm him anymore than I can harm my mate."

Yeah, frustrating. *"Just chill then, I've got this."*

Except this was exactly what I'd waited for, and I barely bit back the need rising within me to hurt him as he'd hurt my people. Only I couldn't go down that road and do the same. I wasn't like him, and I never wanted to be.

Wincrest swiped a hand over his dark beard then eyed Guy. "That would explain the heat, although ensure you return the temperature to normal once you're done. Nice spell."

"Certainly."

"Who is this?" His gaze speared on me.

"My mate, Silvie Moyer."

"You've found your mate? I hadn't heard." A sly grin lifted his lips. "She's a Moyer already? You've wed?"

Yep, I had this. "We did." Hopefully if Wincrest believed we had that would solve one problem. "Guy was rather insistent." Holding out my hand, I showed him the band of gold.

He rubbed his hands together. "I'm well pleased, Guy. Notify Killian, and ensure you receive larger quarters in the barracks." He regarded me. "What skills do you hold, Silvie?"

"Telepathy, teleportation, and…I've yet to discover the rest."

Guy tugged me back to his side. "She's a warrior, a recruit in training. She's yet to go through her rising."

"Make sure you inform me of any further developments then." He squeezed Faith by the shoulders. "How has school been?"

"Not too bad. Finals are close."

"Good. You'll have to accept your role here amongst your people once they're done. I'm off to oversee the games. I'll speak to you later." He shimmered from the room, leaving as quickly as he'd come.

Her shoulders sagged as she faced me. "I think we're running out of time."

"Well, at least I've met him, although what I do to sway his mind is still as much of a mystery as ever."

Guy cleared his throat, his gaze targeted on mine and eyebrows arched to his hairline. "So, now we're married? Would you care to explain?"

"He would have demanded it next. Now that problem is out of the way."

"You should have consulted me."

I tweaked his nose. "I'm sorry, honey. Are you saying you'd like a divorce? Already?"

"Divorce? We just started dating."

Faith stepped past me and dipped one hand in the pool. "This is cooling down on its own, and I'd better get back to Hope. Guy, get Silvie out of here like we discussed." She flashed away.

"Hey, no fair." I turned on Guy. "I'm staying. Don't listen to her."

"She's my princess, and she's right. You can't stay here, not right now." He 'ported us, and we flashed through the dome room then straight to my bedroom.

"I didn't get to see the games."

He opened the door to my sitting room and led me toward my redwood desk piled with papers. "You've missed so much school. You should study, and while that keeps you busy, I'll organize our new quarters. I can't believe we're now wed."

"Do you want a hand?"

"No, I want you to remain here where you're safe." He kissed me, so fiercely my toes tingled. "Be good, and don't forget our deal." He zapped away.

Stupid deal. Still, I'd honor it. I grabbed a sandwich and ate as I slogged through Faith's endless pile of notes. The girls' problem weighed on my mind. Time was running out as Faith had said, and I had to come up with an answer.

As dark descended, I trudged to my dressing room and changed for bed. I had to sort what I could, and fast, which meant plan.

In bed, I played with Guy's mother's ring, twirling it around my finger. Because of the spell Gerritt Moyer had cast, it had brought Guy and me together. Such a beautiful spell, and Gerritt had told me never to forget the fullness of it.

I'd made the sacrifice and committed to being with Guy, to withholding the dome room's location from Davio, Silas, and the rest of my people. I was the fire and Guy was the magic, and together we were one as Moyer. I even understood his fellow warriors in a way I never had before, but—

Guy shimmered into the room. He kicked off his boots and shucked his shirt. "How'd the studying go?"

"Terrible." Oh goodness. His wicked abs were on display. My fingers itched to touch.

He unbuckled his belt and dropped his jeans. Wow, now those were some hot red boxers. Hot. Hot. Hot.

"Why terrible?" He arched a brow.

"Huh?" Had he said something?

"Never mind, with all you've been through I can guess." The bed dipped as he slid under the golden covers. "I've moved my things, and I'll grab some of yours tomorrow and make it look more lived in. You okay with that?"

He'd taken a shower. His black hair was wet and his glorious spicy scent washed over me. "I'm the one who got us married, so I better be."

His breath tickled my cheek as he wrapped his arms around me. "Our lives together have just begun, and since you've agreed to keep the portal's image from any other, so I'll agree not to harm another Peacian. I don't think I even could, not now we're together."

"You no longer hate as you did?" I nuzzled his neck. Clean-shaven. Nice.

"Your heart is so pure, and when you could have harmed Donaldo, you didn't." His lips brushed mine. "I'm going to strive for the same."

"I wanted to hurt him, but I can't be like him. Even your father being behind steel worries me. What do we do about him?" I wish I could do something, anything.

"He'll be freed by my hand, not yours. Although, I've had one thought, but I'll need your help with it."

"You got it."

His gaze lowered to the band of gold around my finger. "Pass me my mother's ring. I'm going to add an enchantment as Dad did, but this time one for him."

"How would that work?" I slipped it off and pressed it into his open palm.

"By using the same endless circle of love he did. Place your hand over mine. We need to seal my mother's ring between us."

"I like your idea. Your mother probably would too." I linked our hands.

"She would have loved to have known you, and I'll be forever grateful for what she did." His eyes sparkled, and then the silver swirled to life. "Where love rises strong, where two souls join for one cause, may fire and magic burn, and all who bear witness be completely drawn. May hate melt away in the blaze of truth, and may freedom be granted for the man who saw to my birth." Leaning in, he kissed me. "I bind this spell to my mother's ring, and through the passage of time to their love which still sings."

Tears welled in my eyes as the ring heated. A warm golden glow shimmered from the small space between our thumbs where our hands didn't quite meet. "T-that was so beautiful."

After it cooled, he took the ring and slipped it onto my finger. "Thank you for aiding me." He pushed me back against the pillows. "Now, for one more thing. It's time to enchant you."

He kissed me, and oh boy, so tantalizingly sweet.

Yeah, my mate had enchanting down to a fine art.

I'd certainly be pestering him for more of this.

Chapter 11

My fingers glowed and I shoved my hands under the cold running water in my bathroom. Not my favorite start to the day, but I couldn't let Guy know I was having problems controlling the heat. He'd confine me to my room, and I'd missed too much school to lose another day.

I flicked off the tap and tugged on my ponytail.

"I'm back, Silvie." Guy rapped on the door.

"Coming." I adjusted the hem of my sunshine-yellow tank top. The white cotton pants were perfect for the spring day. I strode to the door, cool and breezy.

Guy paced my bedroom in hip-hugging black jeans and a red muscle-tee. He tilted his Stetson forward on his head as he eyed me. "Are you sure you're up for school? You're not having any flare-ups?"

"I'm all good, and Faith will be there."

"If there's any sign your fire skill is rising, then 'path me." He snagged my school bag off the end of the bed and slung it over his shoulder.

I eased into his side and 'ported us, not giving him another moment to change his mind. We arrived on the far side of the school field. "You'll be in the outback?"

"Yeah, I'm meeting Maslin there this morning. We've been mustering together." He handed my bag across. "I'll see you later." He kissed me, a grin tugging his lips. "I wish I could take you with me."

"Later. You can show me more of your outback once school's finished."

"You can bet on it. Be careful, and 'path me. I can come in an instant."

"So you said." I backed away. "Go lasso some cows, or toss a spell or two around."

Chuckling, he shimmered and disappeared.

Faith tramped out from behind another tree with dark smudges under her eyes. "Hey."

"What's wrong?" I raced to her side.

"Last night after the games, Nicolas pulled Hope and me aside. He had bad news, although I didn't get any forewarning of it."

"Tell me." I gripped her arms. "You should have told me straight away."

"Yeah, well. Nicolas said while he was speaking to Donaldo during the archery contest, that Killian and Abelard came up to them."

"The slayers." Not good. "Okay, but what's this got to do with Nicolas?"

"He's worried, and for good reason. Killian frankly asked Donaldo if he would grant permission for him to court me. The moment he did, Abelard requested the same with Hope. Nicolas is a healer. He can sense when someone is soul-bound, not that he's ever come right out and asked Hope and me before."

"Did Nicolas say anything else?"

"That Donaldo didn't agree, but that he'd consider their requests."

"Holy moly. We're running out of time."

"There's more." She dropped her head onto my shoulder. "Nicolas didn't hold back. He came right out and asked who Hope and I are mated with."

"What did you say?"

"I told him nothing, and neither did Hope. He left, suspicious."

"We have to talk to him. We can't leave things like that."

"I know, but what's worse is, whenever I focus on Hope and our problem, the silent feedback is deafening. It's like I'm waiting for my forewarning to blare. I couldn't sleep for fear it would."

"Silent feedback? So, there's no new forewarning. That's good, right?"

"You're the key. You've still got this under control."

"Guy's just left for the station. We should organize a meet with Nicolas, one we're all present at, including Hope. We've gotta halt his suspicions before they blow up."

"Let me check on Nicolas first." Her eyes glazed. "Oh, I see him. He's already at the station, talking with Guy and Maslin. Argh, this is becoming impossible."

"I've not met Maslin, but Hope's spoken of him plenty of times." Maslin Sol was distantly related to the girls through their mother's Sol line. Maslin held the same water skill as Hope. The two were close because of their love of the outback.

"Maslin's a part of Hope's inner circle. They're really tight. Maslin was Hope's first choice when Silas first released her."

"Of course." I jumped with excitement, almost knocking her over. Hope and Maslin were almost a thing. Silas complained about Maslin all the time. "Okay, let's look at this from Wincrest's point of view. Ultimately, he wants you and Hope married. He believes neither of you to be mated, and Killian and Abelard have now stated their intentions. If they keep pushing, what'll Wincrest do? Agree. Which is what you saw in your forewarning. We need to circumvent all of that."

"Circumvent is good, except"—her violet gaze narrowed—"why do I feel like I'm going to hate what you're about to say next?"

"Because you are. It goes against the grain for any mated one to be with another, but Hope could date Maslin and make it look real. Which means you'll need to date a warrior too. We just need to figure out whom."

"No way. You did not just say I need to date a warrior."

"Actually, I did."

"Silvie, if Davio or Silas ever found out, Hope and I would be mincemeat."

"Then we'll have to make sure they never find out. It's not like they're in Dralion. How would they ever know you're dating warriors there?"

"I would know." She shivered from head to toe. "Yuck, I don't even want to think about dating another man, let alone touching one."

"You could do it if there wasn't a choice, and right now, there's no choice. You don't want this war to escalate, right?" I squeezed her hands. "C'mon, think about whom you could possibly see yourself trusting, someone Wincrest would give his consent to. We're talking inner circle here."

"There aren't any other warrior men who know of our circumstances. Hope and I have kept the knowledge to a bare few."

"There has to be someone on your radar. A possible match."

She leaned against the tree for support. "The only possibility is Nicolas. He's one of the leading eight, but healers are different. The compassionate side of him is strong. But I can't talk to him, not on my own. What if it all goes wrong?"

"Nicolas is a good choice. I like him, and I'll always be here for you. We stick together." I linked my arm through hers, and without giving her a chance to say no, 'ported us into the glorious, baking heat of the outback.

"Ugh, I feel sick." All color drained from her face. "I don't want to do this."

"I know." I dropped my bag beside the stable's back entrance and helped her remove hers. "Lead the way. Where's Nicolas?"

"You are like the worst best friend ever. I can't believe you're asking me to date another man. After Davio kills me, he'll kill you. So don't say I didn't warn you." She sighed then trudged around the holding corral. Breeding mares swished their tails, and newborn foals pranced up and down the long dusty run. "There he is, out in the field with Guy and Maslin."

"Hey." Hope jogged toward us, her blond hair swinging about her shoulders. "What are you two doing out here?"

Faith hugged her sister. "We're about to fix our problem, or at least try to. How about we walk and talk. Are there any other warriors about?"

"Everyone's out on the range except for those three." She pointed to the men we headed toward. Guy sat on the edge of a water trough, and Nicolas and Maslin stood to the side, all three immersed in their discussion.

I looked at Hope. "Faith told me what Nicolas said to you both, and my plan is we're going to beat Wincrest at his own game."

"What do you mean, beat my grandfather at his own game?"

"Instead of you two having to accept Killian or Abelard, or anyone else who asks Wincrest if they can court you, you're going to take matters into your own hands."

"Ew." She shook her head forcefully. "I already hate the sound of that. I can't believe this is your solution. Silas will kill me if he thinks I'm dating another man, and after me, he'll kill you for suggesting it."

"Death and disaster. Nothing I'm not used to. Anyway, that's why we're not going to tell them. None of us. Not if we all want to live." I kept walking. "Now, I think Maslin will be perfect for you, Hope, provided he agrees to the ruse."

"Silvie, don't you dare tell me I have to date Maslin."

"You have to date Maslin," Faith grumbled as she hooked her arm through Hope's. "And it appears I have to ask Nicolas."

"Nicolas? But he's one of the leading eight. You can't ask him."

"You don't think he's trustworthy, sis?"

"Of course he's trustworthy, but he's still one of the leading eight. I'm not sure he'll agree."

"We don't have time for him to say no." I slipped two fingers between my lips and whistled out. "Hey, boys."

Guy jerked upright, his gaze jumping to me. "What are you doing here?"

I skipped ahead. "If there isn't one problem to fix, there's another. You know me, I'm the problem fixer."

He glanced at my fingers then shot me a confused look.

"No, not that problem. The other one."

"Ah, I see. Then you should have called me for a pickup." He tucked me under his shoulder then turned toward Maslin. "Maslin, meet Silvie, my mate and pest-extraordinaire."

Maslin tipped his stone-colored Stetson toward me. "Nice to meet you, Silvie. Guy was speaking of you just before Nicolas arrived." He switched his gaze to Hope. "Okay, why didn't you tell me what Killian and Abelard said yesterday? Instead, I have to hear about their request to court from Nicolas. Others at the games heard their request too. The news is spreading among the warriors."

"Um, I didn't know how to tell you, but it appears I'm about to now."

"Then get to it. Donaldo believes he has the final say on who you two girls can date. He's about to go too far." Maslin's nostrils flared, his displeasure clear to see. He and Hope were close.

Nicolas eyed Faith and Hope. He looked imposing in his battle leathers. "I haven't told Donaldo you're bound, but you have to come clean. The only question bugging me, is why you haven't already. I thought since you two were so tight with Maslin and Guy, they might know who your mates might be."

Faith wiped her brow. "Ah, we are bound, but we can't speak of our relationships."

"Why not?"

"Can you keep an open mind?"

"Usually."

"Okay, well"—she sucked in a long breath—"our mates aren't from Dralion. Hope and I are bound to protectors, the very men Donaldo would keep us from."

Deathly quiet, he turned his stare on Maslin and Guy. "You two had to have known about this."

Maslin lifted his chin. "We can't deny the girls their mated ones. Even Alexo and Goldie keep their secret from Donaldo."

Nicolas snorted. "That's crazy. They can't be mated to protectors."

"It's the truth." I had to convince Nicolas of our plan. "Hope is mated to my brother, and Faith to my cousin."

"What? Hold on. Are you saying you're a Peacian?" His gaze jolted to Guy. "Is this the truth? You're mated to a Peacian as well?"

"Silvie's loyal to the girls and me. She'd never speak of what she knows, nor give our portal away."

"She's still a Peacian."

"Nicolas, she's also my best friend." Faith wrapped an arm around my shoulders. "We've known each other our entire lives, and as Maslin said, Alexo and Goldie keep our secret. Dad and our aunt have given us free choice, but we take extreme care. In Peacio, my mate's family and closest also know and keep it to themselves."

"Who exactly is your mate?" Nicolas thumped his chest. "Do I even want to know?"

"Davio Loveria."

"What? You're mated to Peacio's prince?"

"Yes, and Hope is mated to Silas Carver."

"What the hell." His face turned bull-fighting red.

"Calm down." Maslin gripped Nicolas's shoulder. "They're mated, and to two men who would die to protect them. That's what's going on. When Hope was searching for answers about her mother's lost heritage, her journey led her to No-Man's Land. Goldie, Guy and I were there with her, as were Davio and Silas. Their mates wouldn't allow any harm to come to them, and now you have to decide if that's what you want too."

"I can't. I'm one of the leading eight. My position will be in jeopardy if I withhold this."

"Prince Alexo knows. You don't think Donaldo's son doesn't jeopardize more?"

"Nicolas." I stepped up to him. "You healed me, a Peacian. Faith and Hope are your princesses, and they need your aid. You can't walk away from them, not when we need to buy them some time. We need more from you than simple withholding."

"I can't believe this. What exactly are you asking?"

I was the key. I could do this. I had to convince him of the plan. "We need you to step in as Faith's boyfriend. In front of Wincrest, you have to appear as if the two of you are together." I glanced at Maslin. "We need you to come in to bat for Hope."

"You don't even have to ask." Maslin swung around to Hope. "Whatever you need, I'll be there."

"Thank you." Her bottom lip trembled. "Silas can't know. He'd never be able to handle this news."

"He won't hear a thing from me."

She sniffed and hugged him. "This means so much to me."

Faith rubbed Hope's back then turned her gaze on Nicolas. "I know Silvie said I need your help, but I'd never force you to give it. All I ask is that you keep our secret as Guy and Maslin do."

He ground his heel into the hard-packed soil. "I'll speak to

Alexo and Goldie first. I'll give you my answer once I have. If that's all, I need to leave." He flashed away. So fast.

"He really didn't take that very well. I'll just make sure he's doing what he said." Faith's eyes glazed over as she activated her forethought.

Guy gripped my hand. "I didn't want to tell you this, but your fingertips are glowing."

"What?" The tips weren't yet alight, but close, very close. "No. No. No. I don't have time for this right now."

"Think cold stuff. This is the outback, Silvie. One spark can set fire to what little grass is left and race across miles within minutes."

I conjured a snow field, one with a fresh fall, only my fingers still glowed. "Damn, I'll think of something else."

"You have the fire skill?" Maslin gaped. "That hasn't been seen in generations."

"She does, and her rising is close." Guy clasped Maslin's arm. "Thanks for your support just now."

"Anytime."

"I'll dip my hands in water." I leaned into the water trough. Great. Bone dry, the base caked with a layer of rock-hard dirt. "Well, that's not very helpful."

"There's plenty of water at the river." Maslin nodded at Guy. "If you take her there, I'll keep the other station hands busy." He flashed away.

Hope stepped forward. "I'll come and douse her if needed." She grabbed Faith's hand and squeezed. "How's it going with Nicolas?"

She blinked and cleared her sight. "He's with them now in Dad's study. There's nothing more we can do." She fanned her face and stared at me. "You're getting hot again."

"I can't stop it."

"Then let's get to the river now." She flashed away with Hope. I followed her airstream and Guy arrived hard on my tail.

Wow. Gone was the barren red dirt and instead fields of green surrounded a mighty river. It throbbed with life. Ducks and birds took flight along the waterway, sweeping low into the rushes either side with a cacophony. And far into the distance, thousands of head of cattle grazed. Now, this was the outback as it should be.

Hope removed her Stetson and the breeze lifted the sweaty strands of her blond hair from her face. "Here Maslin and I use our water skill. We drive the water further inland from the river during the controlled river releases. This area is alive, Silvie, so take care and don't set fire to it."

"I'll do my best."

Faith bent at the river's edge, scooped a handful. "Let's cool you down, Silvie." She tossed the water over my sandaled feet. Steam gushed into the air. "Whoa, you are very, very hot."

The lush grass at my feet curled. "Maybe this isn't the best place for me."

"It is." Guy motioned toward Hope. "Let's see you in action. More water is needed. That's all."

"No." I backed away. "I can't stand Hope's kind of action. I'll just dip my fingers in like Faith did."

"You don't have a choice. You're getting hotter by the second and we need to cool you down." With a sweeping motion of her hands toward the river, Hope made waves ripple. Through her skill alone, a huge mass rose, bubbling around the edges until the water poured in on itself. She drew it into a controlled orb.

A pool-full of water, and far more than she needed to cool me down, levitated over the river toward me. "Hey, that's not even remotely funny. Stop that."

Faith sighed. "It has to happen."

"Let's think of another way." I darted further back, but the rolling sphere soared to block the sun.

"Stay still," Hope warned.

I ducked and ran, only Guy caught me and swung me

around. "What are you doing? Let me go. You're supposed to be on my side."

"You have to cool down, and this is the only way. I'm going to help." His beautiful enchanter eyes swirled. "With legs of lead, you will stand still. Let this spell take hold so no harm can be—"

I shoved a hand over his mouth. "Don't even think about finishing that spell."

A deluge hit me, sluicing over my head and down my body until it pooled in a hissing puddle at my feet. Guy jumped clear of the hot water with a yelp.

Uncontrollable fire flared at my fingertips. "Um, that should have stopped that."

"You have to stop the flames, or I will," Hope yelled. She flicked her fingers and another large pool of water rose from the river.

"Put that back. I can't get control under this kind of duress." I glared at Faith. "Tell her to stop."

"Hope has a mind of her own, and you must be moving into your rising." She jerked back. "You've gotta rein in your temper. Every time it flares, so does your heat. It pulses in waves."

My anger surged and the grass around me rippled, flattened and became browned.

"I've got this." Hope's bubble of water shot at me. It knocked me onto my butt.

I spat out a mouthful of sandy yuck. "Okay, that's enough."

"I've barely started." She collected another rolling sphere, and I so wasn't going to stick around for that.

I 'ported, and fast. In my dressing room, I grabbed my red swimsuit and whipped it on. I'd take matters into my own hands, and if I needed water, I'd make sure it suited me.

"Silvie, I know you're in there. The wood's warping and the doorknob is half melted." Guy thumped the door. "We've gotta get you somewhere safe."

"I'm heading to the underground cavern. The pools are private and hot. Hot water I don't mind. Get Faith to bring you. She has the 'porting image." Fire sparked from my fingertips. I had to go.

Within moments I was there, my feet sinking into fine gray sand. Nice. Warm air filled the cavern, and a mist hovered over the large pool of clear water. Dark rocks lined the sides, and a small tunnel of light tracked in from one of the overhead vents. Cozy.

I could do this. I walked in, and even though hot, the water still bubbled. The mist thickened as steam continued to rise. I moved deeper. The water rose to my hips, my chest, and then flowed over my shoulders.

"Silvie? Are you in here? Damn it, I can't see a thing."

"Don't come in, Guy." Bubbles burst all around as I dove under, and the water, so hot, soothed my skin. I broke the surface.

"Air so thick, disperse and spread," Guy chanted. "Let me see my mate, the one whose fire flares red." The air cleared and his gaze locked on mine. Faith and Hope, having changed into their swimsuits, stood with him. "There you are. I'll spell the water and try and cool it."

"I like it like this."

"And I can't get in. I'm spelling it."

"You okay, Silvie?" Hope peered at me. "I 'pathed Silas. He and Davio are on their way. They won't let you go through your rising alone. None of us will."

"I'm coming in." Guy stripped off his shirt and tossed it behind him. "Where there's heat, let it fade. Allow more than one to bathe." His gaze bored into mine as he shucked off his boots and black jeans.

Left in cotton shorts, the blazing color of the sun, my temperature hurtled upward again. Bubbles burst to the surface in a gurgling riot. "You're going to have to spell stronger than that, or else stay out."

"Where my mate heats, counteract with cool. Diffuse and chill, within a moment's pull." He dove in and emerged nose to nose before wrapping his arms around me. "Don't ever run like that from me again."

"Then don't spell me when you know I won't like it."

"I have to keep you safe."

"That doesn't mean getting me wet."

"You're wet now." He kissed me, and every cell in my body reared for more. Oh, sweet heaven. His mouth was hot, and his body pressed against mine even hotter.

Such scalding heat.

"Whoa." He jerked back, swinging his hand back and forth through the water. "Hold on. Another flare-up."

"Of course she'll have flare-ups if you're that close." Hope swam in beside him. "Emotions run at three-times the strength as well. You two shouldn't touch during her rising. It'll only make things harder for her."

Silas shimmered into the room in his trunks. "Hey, sis. I got the call. Your rising's here?"

"Yep, and about time you showed up." I didn't want to do this without my brother. He'd always been there for the big stuff, and this was considered big stuff.

Silas swam out and caught Hope around the waist. "Not too close to the hot-headed one, love." His gaze veered to Guy. "I didn't expect to see you here, Moyer. Last I heard, Silvie was after a final farewell."

"It didn't happen, and it never will. Where she is, will be where you'll find me."

"Damn, it was the meal, wasn't it? I should have spiked the food before she took it."

Guy's gaze lit on mine. "As my father's spell said, I'll never go hungry before her."

Silas coughed. "Ah, excuse me, that'll do."

I laughed as Guy circled in behind me. "I take it you want to get burnt again?"

"I can't help myself. It's just as well I fast-heal." He slid his hands over my hips, nestled his chin on my shoulder. "Look ahead. It looks like Loveria is here too, and ready for a swim," he whispered in my ear.

"Moyer," Davio gritted out, having 'ported in. "What are you doing here?"

Faith grabbed his hand. "Hey, don't get upset, but they're staying together."

"What happened to their release?"

"They took it back."

"Silvie, is he truly the one you want? Feel free to say no."

Poor Davio. "Yep, without a doubt he's the one I want."

"Great," he sighed as he eyed Silas. "Sorry I'm late, but when you said it was Silvie's rising, I dropped by the stockpile of logs in the forest. It's all set to burn if she needs it."

Oooh, he had a stockpile of logs? Yay. "I love you, cousin."

"Only use it if necessary, Silvie." Davio met Guy's gaze. "Every time my cousin's needed you, you've been there. In my opinion that's what counts, whether you're a warrior or not."

Faith flung water as she wrapped her arms around Davio's neck. "Now, that's why I love you. Your heart is open to change."

He cupped her cheek. "I'm learning my enemy isn't exactly the enemy anymore, and it's because of you. Times are a-changing."

Silas inclined his red-gold head toward Guy. "There are warriors in our midst as never before, as there are protectors in yours. Can you handle it, Moyer?"

"In the past we've battled, and I don't deny the hate which festers within the hearts of Dralion's people, but it is a hate which must go." His gaze flicked to Davio's. "Because of Silvie, I understand this war needs to come to an end. She's loyal to you and your people, and I would never compromise that loyalty, not when it makes her who she is. A nurturer, even with the greatest of the battle skills."

"How do you believe this war should come to an end, Moyer?" Davio joined Silas, and the two stood united as water lapped at their chests, the girls digging their heels in beside them.

"I'm loyal to Donaldo, but I also understand we must work together. One warrior and one protector at a time. We have to see peace prevail."

My heart pounded. His loyalty was strong, and one warrior and one protector at a time sounded like a good strategy to me. "Guy, I like what you just said. It sounds like a plan."

"It does, and we certainly need one." He pressed my hands to his chest. "Together we're stronger as one."

"We always will be." I glanced at Davio. "What do you think? We have to try and make this work."

"It's good. Working together, one warrior and one protector at a time. I like it. We could turn the tide and make a change."

"I love it." Faith almost bowled him over as she hugged him. "This is exactly what Hope and I have wanted. For peace to prevail between our nations. Having a plan like this is a start."

"Yes. Yes. Yes." Hope kissed Silas. "We're loyal to our own people, but we're also loyal to each other. We can do this. Already there're us and our inner circles. We just have to keep extending our reach. The more people on our side, the better."

I looked deep into Guy's eyes, seeing the depth of his need. He wanted this, just as much as I did. "This is what your father would want too. He said so few Magiolings are finding their mated ones. Our skills continue within our family lines, but they don't return to full strength unless we're born of the mated bond. And we all know that. It's also been centuries since my fire skill was seen, and you're one of few left who enchant. Your father's right in saying we're losing the battle, and it's with ourselves more than any other. Just imagine when we can all live openly with our mates. When our secrets are gone." Oooh, yes. My blood heated at the thought.

"Love, that sounds—" He lurched back. "This rising really sucks, and you're getting too hot to handle. I'll spell again."

Silas lifted Hope from the water. "Sis, really? You need to cool it. And could you please keep your distance from Moyer? It would be helpful."

"Maybe Silvie should go for a swim," Hope interjected. "So her energy distributes in other ways. I'll come with you, Silvie. I have a gel which coats my skin. It's part of my skill and kicks in when I'm diving deep in the ocean. It insulates me from the cold, but I don't see why it can't insulate me against your heat." Her skin shimmered with the slippery gel, and she slid out of Silas's arms, escaping him with ease. She swam around me.

Having someone swim with me would be good. I wanted my closest near.

She popped up then ran her palm down her arm. "Oh, it works like a treat. The gel melts away, but my skin produces it again just as quickly. I'll have to watch my hydration, but I can do this. Let's swim together."

I blew Guy a kiss and followed her out into the deep, only I'd barely begun to swim when a wave of heat shot through my veins. On my back, I lifted my hands free of the water and pointed upward. Fire blasted out and hit the rocky ceiling.

Beautiful. Such a glorious explosion of red, burnt orange and sizzling yellow.

"Silvie!"

I grinned at Guy's shout. "Don't you like it, honey?"

He let out a long sigh. "Get some control. There's only so much I can spell at once, and now I have to cool the ceiling before it collapses on us. Aim for the walls if you have to."

"Oh, good idea. The walls." My fingers tingled to release more fire.

"Give me a second first to work out a spell for the roof." He rubbed his forehead. "Okay, hopefully this will work. Take the rising steam and along the ceiling of rock, layer and lock it into ice. I need prisms of white, and I need them spun nice." His words floated to me, and above, the steam crystalized across the ceiling, adding layer upon layer of the tough white stuff.

"Okay, ice opposes fire. Now for the walls." Guy glanced at Faith. "You should be forewarning me of these problems before they arise."

"There aren't any forewarnings. You're dealing with them first, but I'll certainly holler if you slip up anywhere." Her brow furrowed. "Hey, what was your rising like? I'm trying to imagine how that would work for an enchanter."

"Nobody could stop the barrage of rhymes which spilled from my mouth. I did a number of terrible things whenever somebody attempted to contain me. It wasn't pretty." He shifted his gaze toward Hope, who now bobbed in the water, waiting for me to catch her up. A look passed between them.

"You were there." I kicked toward her. "What did he do?"

"It was unbelievable. He turned me completely purple. Skin, hair, everything, and all because he liked the color of my violet eyes and thought the rest of me should match."

I laughed. "No way."

"Yes way."

Silas chuckled from where he'd clambered onto a large rock at the water's edge, no doubt to get a better view of Hope. "I would have loved to have seen that, Moyer. Can you do it again to my mate?"

Hope gasped. "Silas, not funny. And no, Guy won't. Not if he values his life."

Pushing a hand through his slick black hair, Guy said, "It took me a couple of days to figure out how to reverse the spell, and I've learnt my lesson. No one messes with a Wincrest."

I kicked away from Hope as another wave of heat pulsed

through my veins. "Guy, this one's gonna be bad." I aimed my fingers at the wall. "Can you get that now?"

"One sec." He mumbled a short ditty, and ice shimmered over the surface of the walls as my fire flared.

It slammed into the layer of ice and blasted off. Chunks of pristine white flew and everyone ducked. "Stay low. My rising is definitely rising."

"You've gotta swim." Having dove off the boulder, Silas swung back onto the top of it. "Force your energy out, but not through your fire. There are other ways. Use them."

"Sorry." Yeah, I had to get busy and swim. I had to move and get the energy out that way. Kicking, I swam length after length as Hope dipped in and around, remaining solidly at my side.

She was fast, sleeker than a seal in her element and clearly having a world of fun, yet no matter how hard I kicked, my energy grew. It surged, and I battled my natural response to keep it in check.

Still, I did what I could, but as the hours passed, my fire bubbled and brewed, stewing beyond my control.

"You're getting worse," Guy called out. "I can barely keep up with your demand. The ice is melting from your heat alone."

Energy rippled through me, only seconds after the last flare. I had no time to warn him and sent the explosive fireball upward. Fire lit the craggy ceiling. Sharp black rock sheared off and shot in all directions.

I couldn't keep doing this. Someone would get hurt. I swam toward Davio. "It's time for the bonfire. I'll trail your airstream."

"Done." He nodded and flashed away.

I followed, fast.

Chapter 12

Pine needles stuck to the wet soles of my feet. The clearing in the forest was dark, the sun having dipped below the horizon hours ago. A stockpile of logs awaited its fate. Beautiful. My kind of kindling.

"You're glowing, Silvie." Davio hunkered down, one hand pressed to the damp soil. Faith flashed in beside him and knelt with one hand on his back. Silas blinked in with Hope.

"Where's Guy?"

He shimmered in. "I barely caught the others' airstream."

"No, stay back, okay? I don't want you getting hurt." Fire pulsed from my raised fingertips. It vaulted right over his shoulder.

He ducked. "Hell, the flames are moving up your arms. Your fire is spreading."

Flames raced to my shoulders and across my chest. The fire swept down, around my hips, thighs and legs. My toes tingled as fire flared from the tips. I was ablaze, every inch of me. Sooo mesmerizing.

"Everyone, back to the tree line," Davio yelled. The others sought the shelter they needed, all except Guy. He remained crouched, and close.

"You can't handle this kind of heat. Go. I'll be fine, Guy."

"No. I'm not leaving your side. You're my mate. You need

me."

"I've never lit up like this."

"Send the fire from you. You have to release this excess energy. Aim it at the stockpile."

My blood fairly sang as I zeroed in on it. It was all for me.

Oh yeah, this was what I wanted. To burn.

In anticipation, I stamped my feet, only a ripple of fire flared out from my toes. It sent an undulating wave of heat across the ground. Smoke puffed and clouded around.

Guy fanned the air. "Don't set fire to the ground. The stockpile."

My heart burst with a hunger for more. "This is amazing."

He edged closer, almost touching my flames. "Keep your focus, and your sight on the prize."

"The prize. Yes." Arms raised, I spread my palms toward the tower of logs. My blood exploded with heat, and fire crackled and popped in a sizzling rampage. My flames lit the night sky. Wow, this was one seriously hot skill.

"Let the heat go!" Guy bellowed.

Go. Yes. I drew every last ounce of energy and brought it forth. The flames pulsing from me grew thicker, stronger, and brighter. The red flickered with blue then a cold, dark thing shoved all my feelings aside. Burn. I had to burn and devour.

"Silvie, no!" Someone slammed into me, only I was rooted to the ground by the sheer force of the energy bound within. "I've got you. Now, damn it, send the fire from you."

Guy. I couldn't harm him. My mate. With my last reserves, I thrust the build-up to my hands. I shot the fire like an arrow into the heart of the logs. It hit with a thunderous roar and flames soared into the sky, spearing out in a deadly array.

"Don't let me go." My energy drained from one heartbeat to the next. My limbs went rubbery and my body became a dead weight.

"Never. We stick together." He scooped me up before I

sank to the ground. "You did it. You managed not to burn me and your fire is out. Your rising is done."

My vision swam, and I dropped my head onto his shoulder. My energy was completely gone, every last ounce sapped. Had I really done it? "Is everyone all right?"

"After that show, just." Faith bounded in.

"It was spectacular." Davio grinned. "There're a few fires flaring up of course, but with Hope's help we'll deal with them."

"Way to go, sis." Silas kissed my cheek.

"I'm needed out there to bring water in, but congratulations." Hope rubbed my back.

"Be careful. No one's allowed to get burnt while they put my fires out."

"We'll get onto it now." Silas pulled Hope into his arms and flashed away with her. Davio and Faith followed in their airstream.

I looked deep into Guy's eyes. My enchanter who would forever enchant me. "Thank you for staying. You were amazing."

He pressed his lips to mine, his kiss filled with more emotion than I could grapple. "I wouldn't be anywhere else. You're my world, my heart and my soul."

"As you are mine." I kissed him back.

Slowly, he pulled away, ending our kiss far too soon. "I'd better get you to bed so you can rest."

"Yes, please. That sounds—" He 'ported us into my bathroom. "Fast."

"I'm all spelled-out. It was exhausting keeping up with you today." He set me on my feet between him and the shower then reached inside the stall and flicked on the lever. With one hand, he tested the heat. "Okay, this is good."

"I don't know if I need any more water today. I'm water-logged."

"It's piping hot. You'll love it." He carried me in. Steam

enveloped us as he propped me against his side. Gently, he lathered a bar of soap then smoothed his hands over my arms and around my neck. "Tip your head back."

I did, and he plopped shampoo onto the top and massaged it in. "Oh, that's nice. You have magic fingers."

"You scared me out there when you were on fire. You had no control."

"It felt amazing to wield that much energy." I washed the suds from my hair and slumped against the shower wall in my swimsuit. "Not that I have much now."

"Here, I've got you." He shut the water off and bundled me in a fleecy yellow towel. In my dressing room, he lowered me to my feet before my dresser. "I'll wait outside."

"I'll be quick." I changed into a pair of pink sleep shorts and a white tank top then dragged open the door.

"Let's get you into bed. You look ready to drop." He set a hand at my waist and guided me to bed.

I crawled in and let out the loudest sigh as my head hit the pillow. I would never have envisioned this day. Having the fire skill rocked. "I want to thank you properly."

"You already have, but more sounds good to me." He kissed me, his hot lips scorching mine. "Is this the kind of thanks you had in mind?"

"Yep." Oh boy. I'd never be able to get enough of his kisses. "You have magic lips too."

He flicked off the overhead light then returned to nibble his way along my jaw and down my neck. "That's because I now have a very fiery muse."

"As I have my very own enchanter." I stretched as he sucked my skin and drew it deep between his lips. "Are you giving me a hickey?"

"A big red one on your neck. Your favorite color. You can take a look at it in the morning."

I sank deeper into the mattress and wriggled as my need for

him intensified. "Well, don't stop. This is my kind of rest."

"Silvie." He whispered my name as he nipped his way to the other side of my neck. "I can't stand the thought of being apart from you."

"Me, either." I pushed my fingers deep into his silky black hair. "I can't even believe we tried to end things."

He groaned and sucked on a new spot.

"If you need me to give up culinary—"

"No." He lifted his head and a touch of moonlight tracing through the crack in the curtains played over his strong jaw and high cheek bones. It lit the silver in his eyes. "You'll never give up anything for me. We have our telepathic link, and it takes no time at all for me to get to you."

"Or for me to get to you." I clasped his face between my hands. "So it's settled?"

"Is what settled?"

"I can come to you as necessary too. The station and Dralion are safe places. How can they not be, once news spreads we're together?"

"I'll only agree to the station since Hope and Maslin are there most of the time. You don't travel to Dralion unless it's with me." He lowered his head, blew warm air across my neck. "Excuse me. But I'm on a mission, a very covert one."

I laughed as I held him close. And it surely was a mission he didn't deviate from.

My warrior was wise, clever and very, very sneaky.

* * * *

Yawning, I rolled and bumped into Guy's solid back. He lay on his front, one cheek pressed into his pillow.

I snuck a look at the time. Whoa. 8:30 AM.

I bolted out of bed. "Guy, I have school, like now." I ran for the dressing room and right into him. He'd 'ported that fast.

"Let's get one thing straight." Not quite yet awake, he rubbed the sleep from his eyes. "From now on, our mornings begin with a kiss."

I tapped my watch. "School starts n—"

He claimed his kiss, and with the same utter precision he'd done in giving me hickeys. "Okay, now you can go." He grinned and swatted my bottom.

I wobbled as I shut the dressing room door. That man knew how to kiss, and yay, he was all mine.

I wriggled into a pair of denim cutoffs then tugged on a molten-red, scoop-necked blouse. I zapped to my bathroom and finger-combed my hair. The mirror showed a mess, but it would have to do. I jammed my favorite clip into the side to keep the worst of the wayward red-gold mess at bay then with no time left, flashed to school.

I ran hard across the field and toward the mathematics block.

Almost out of breath, I dashed down the corridor. Just ahead, the last of the students hiked it into class. Phew. Made it.

Faith pushed off the wall next to the lockers in loose tan cargo pants and a slim white t-shirt. She tossed me my school bag. "You know how to cut it fine. I went and fetched this from the station this morning."

"Thank you." I squeezed her hard. "You're a life-saver."

"No problem. Mr. Houghton's almost here." She snatched my wrist and dragged me into class behind her. Next to the windows, we took the last two spare desks.

"I'm just making sure you're okay." Guy's voice held longing as it bounced inside my head.

"Yep. I got to class in the nick of time."

"I'll be there to pick you up after school."

"Sure, you do that, just in case I've forgotten the way home and all."

"Don't be cheeky."

"You've barely seen cheeky. I'll talk to you later." Someone bumped the leg of my chair from behind as I closed the link.

"Hey, how's the firecracker?"

I scraped the chair around, and with a grin, grabbed Belle's hand. "You missed my rising."

"I know, but I heard all about it this morning from Davio and Silas at breakfast. Congratulations." She inclined her head toward Zayn, who sat alertly next to her. "You've got two additional sets of eyes today. Silas wanted the extra support after all that happened yesterday."

"Thanks." I nudged my foot against Zayn's. "You need to slump a little if you want to blend in."

He scooted down in his chair and kicked his feet out to the side. "That better?"

"A bit. You didn't bring your dagger with you?" It was hard for our protectors to go anywhere without a weapon.

"No, and I feel naked without it. I always have one concealed on my wrist." He adjusted the long sleeves of his black-and-white-paneled shirt.

"I have something that you don't need to conceal, and it's pointy." Rummaging through my bag, I found a pen.

"Ha, that is not a dagger."

"It'll still keep your hands busy." I tossed him a pad too. "Did you hear my mate is here to stay?"

"Yeah, I got the update. I guess now I'll have to get used to him."

Belle slid her elbows onto her desk, rested her chin in her open palms. "I want to hear exactly what made you change your mind, and don't miss a detail."

A wave of satisfaction rolled through me. As an empath, she would have liked that. "We worked it out."

"Argh, give me more. That emotion was not enough. I like hearing all the good, gooey stuff."

Faith flicked one of my loose locks and it bounced up and hooked over the end of my nose. "I'll give you the goopy scoop later, Belle."

I flipped the lock away as the door whooshed open. Mr. Houghton walked in. With a quick survey of the class, he lowered his pile of papers to his desk. "Open your textbooks everyone. We'll begin at page one-hundred and twenty. Paragraph three." He headed to his treasured whiteboard with his black marker in hand and scribbled across the board's surface.

"Hey," I whispered to Faith. "Any word from Nicolas?"

She opened her textbook and flipped to the right page then set the book between us. "No, and look busy. We don't need detention slips for nattering."

I picked up my pen and tapped her nose. "Righto, busy. We'll chat later. I haven't forgotten your problem."

I read from the text.

Yuck, calculus. How boring.

The rest of the day was just as tedious. Mrs. Gray requested I join her special English lunchtime tutorial.

Nice of her.

Then after last period's PE, I left the girls' changing rooms with Faith and Belle, completely exhausted.

Zayn waited ahead for us under the shade of an umbrella tree in the small cobbled quad next to the fenced school pool. "Girls." He tilted his head toward us. "What's on the agenda now?"

"Homework, and I've already had enough of school work today." I wriggled my fingers in front of his nose. "Look, no unexpected fire either. You can report to Silas and Davio I was a model student."

He chuckled then stopped as his gaze bolted over my head. "Ah, your warrior is here, and it appears he's brought company."

I swiveled around. Shoot. Nicolas was here, and in full battle leathers.

Belle swayed into me. "Oh my goodness, that other warrior...wow."

"Wow?" She did not just say *wow*.

"I—I—" She fluttered her hand over her chest. Her gaze danced over Nicolas as he approached.

Why was Belle reacting this way? I studied Nicolas. He skidded to a stop and thumped his chest. His gaze jerked toward Belle then zeroed in on her.

Faith gripped Zayn's arm. "Forewarning. Get Belle out of here. Now."

"I'm on it." He snagged Belle around the waist and flashed away. So fast.

"What's going on?"

"I'll tell you later." She tugged me toward the men. "Let's deal with one forewarning at a time."

Nicolas eyed Faith as he stepped up to her. "Who was that?"

"Who do you mean?" She scratched the back of her neck.

The woman with the long locks and deep brown eyes."

"Oh, you noticed her, huh?"

"She had a dimple each side of her mouth, and a mole above her left eyebrow."

Faith wiped her forehead. "Yep, you noticed her all right. Belle's a protector, an empath, one in the know."

"Damn." Arms crossed, he drew his dark brows together.

Heck, Nicolas had noticed Belle just as greatly as Belle had noticed him. Could he be her mate? The one who'd never—

"I came because I've made my decision." Nicolas nodded. "Alexo and Goldie were adamant your secret and Hope's be kept. I've considered everything presented to me, and I'm in agreement."

"You are?" Faith let out a shuddering breath. "My father protected my mother's whereabouts for eighteen years when he knew Donaldo would never have accepted her Earthling status."

"Yes, he told me, and of Hope's journey in discovering your mother's true Magioling heritage. He spoke of all those lost years, and the pain he endured. Already so many of our people suffer the same loss of their mated one because of the dome. As it is, you and Hope are full-blooded, and if Donaldo hadn't forced your parents' separation, then you wouldn't have had to live here on Earth, but in your rightful place. I'm in accord, that you and I will provide a united front before Donaldo." He leaned in, kissed her cheek. "It seems we're dating."

"Thank you." She hugged him, tears slipping down her cheeks. "You and Maslin are amazing, and you won't regret your decision."

"We better not. We'll make this work, somehow." He rubbed her back and glanced at Guy. "We'll catch you later. Faith and I need some time to plan." He zapped away with her.

Guy pulled me into his arms. "Hey, you're crying."

"I am?" I wiped my eyes, finding my cheeks wet. "This is such a relief. Everything has hinged on finding an answer, and Nicolas and Maslin stepping up provides part of it."

"They still have to convince Donaldo, and then there's Killian and Abelard to get around." He tipped up my chin. "Alexo's arranged a formal dinner for tonight. He wants to ensure Donaldo sees the girls with Nicolas and Maslin. It begins with pre-dinner drinks at five sharp. We're all expected."

My heart skipped a beat. The dreaded Wincrest and the slayers in one room. Great. Yet this was what it was all about. Faith's forewarning. "That doesn't give us much time."

"Yes, we need to get ready. You also have to put your clothes away."

"My clothes? What do you—"

Everything darkened as he 'ported us. We passed through the stinky dome room and straight to his new quarters. "While you were at school, I moved some of your things here."

A large pile of my clothing lay strewn over a king-sized bed covered in a thick white comforter. Plush red pillows rested against the graceful curve of the wooden headboard. "You got a new bed?"

He grinned. "Yeah, you broke the old one, and it was my favorite out of the two. What do you think of the desk?" A chunky oak desk held two wonky piles of very familiar looking cookbooks. "The books are copies of the same ones you had in your sitting room. I found replicas on Earth."

"You did?" I lifted the top volume and thumbed through it. Yellow squares of paper marked several pages. "What are these for?"

Brushing up behind me, he skimmed my hips with his hands. "You're welcome to make anything I've marked, and anytime you'd like."

"Hmm, southern fried chicken and corn and cheese bread." I flicked to his next marking. "Mama Maria's meatballs in spicy sauce." Continuing through, I hit the desserts, and almost every page in that section was marked. "Interesting. I think there's only one you've missed. What's wrong with the caramelized apples flambéed?"

He nuzzled my ear. "Knowing you, you won't want to put the flambé out."

"Good point." I laughed and set the book down.

"Did you see the bed?"

"You know I"—he swung me into his arms and dropped me across the pillows—"did."

One serious expression darkened his eyes as he crawled in overtop. "You must be careful with what you say at this dinner. The entire leading eight will be there."

"Okay, why don't you prepare me?" I wrapped my arms around his neck.

"If anyone asks you a sensitive question, direct it back at me."

"I can do that."

"Don't burn any of them." He kissed me, nipping softly at my lips. "No matter if you want to."

"No fair."

"Let's hang your clothes before we run out of time." He swept me onto my feet. "We have a dressing room." Scooping an armful, he inclined his head toward one of the two side rooms. "It's not much, but it's more than I've ever had before."

"I had no problem with your last room. You and I being together is what matters."

He led the way and added my clothes to the rail opposite his. The space was small, but just perfect. I snuggled against his back. "I like our new quarters."

"We need to get moving." He backed out then returned with another armful of clothing and speedily hung each piece.

"There's still enough time, and slow down. Did you bring all my clothes?"

"Half. I didn't want anyone to question you lived here. I'm going to take a shower while you finish putting your things away." He raced off to the bathroom.

What was his rush? I knocked on the bathroom door. "Guy, there's moving, and then there's moving. Is there something you're not telling me? What's wrong?"

"I'm nervous about tonight."

"Faith would have told us if there's a problem."

"Sometimes her forewarning gives next to no time. I don't want anything to go wrong."

Well, he had a point there. Faith rarely gave much notice, but that's because people had free will, and our futures were always in flux. I trudged to the bed and sorted the last of the clothes. I pulled out a slinky white dress and nude-colored heels to wear for the night.

I shimmied into the tight number and smoothed it into place. With a little adjustment to the side-split, the fit was perfect.

The bathroom door opened and a rush of steam escaped. Guy stood in the doorway, a fleecy blue towel slung low on his hips. Water dripped from his dark locks onto his wide shoulders and trickled down his chest.

I adored his chest. "Okay, you better get dressed before I take a bite out of you."

"That dress—" He gripped the edge of the doorjamb. "You have to change."

"Because…" I glanced down. It was an evening gown, one I'd worn to formal dinners at the castle. I liked it.

"I'll never keep my hands off you in that." He stumbled to his dressing room and shut the door with a loud clunk.

"Well, that's really not an issue for me." I knocked on his dressing room door. "Are you all right? Your nervousness is going rub off on me if you're not careful."

"The bathroom's all yours," he yelled back.

"Well, that's obvious." Ha, men. I headed there and searched the vanity drawers for his brush. Instead I found mine and my favorite gold hair clasps. He'd also brought various bits and pieces of my makeup, enough to do an admirable job for the night.

Using a hand towel, I rubbed the steamy mirror clear and eyed my reflection. My cheeks were too pink, so I dabbed foundation on and covered the freckles. I tidied my hair and secured a clasp at each side. Some lippy, and I was done.

"Are you ready?" Guy, dressed in pressed black pants and a starched, white-collared shirt, looked deliciously edible. The golden tie around his neck sizzled with color.

Oh, I wanted my mate. Advancing on him, I grinned. "I am now."

"You didn't change." His gaze roamed my body as he backed out of the room. "You should change."

"I like the way you look at me in this. I'm keeping it on." I sashayed toward him and lifted my arms, only he grabbed them and kept a firm foot between us.

"Silvie, without my father, you're my only family, no matter it's an act before Donaldo. Having you here, and your things..." He looked deep into my eyes. "I can't lose you, not now, not ever." Lowering to one knee, he clasped my right hand tightly.

"Whoa. What are you doing?" I tried to yank him up. He wouldn't budge.

"Her man will bow down, and shall never go hungry before her."

"The last part of your father's spell."

"Yes." He dug into his pocket and pulled out a red velvet box.

"What are you—" No, he couldn't be doing that.

He flicked open the lid and turned the box toward me. Cocooned within was an impressive square-cut diamond, glittering bright.

"This can't be happening."

"I love you, Silvie." His gaze, so focused, drained the remaining air from my lungs. "With my heart and soul. Finally I'm living again, because of you. Don't make me hunger. I want you as my wife."

My legs wobbled and I gripped his shoulders to keep from slithering to the floor. "I love you too. So much, it hurts when we're not together."

"Is that a yes?" He rose to his feet and lifted me off mine. "Please, tell me that's a yes."

"If it is, we're going to have a very long engagement."

"What about a week?" His smiling lips came down on mine. He kissed me, long and deeply, until my legs went to mush.

"A year sounds better," I finally got out.

"I could do a month." He grinned and slipped the ring over my knuckle to join his mother's gold band.

"Holy moly. I can't believe I'm agreeing to this." I turned my hand side to side. The diamond dazzled with its brightness. "Silas is going to freak when he sees this. You better make sure you remain armed for some time to come. This is the last thing he'll expect."

"I'll speak to him."

"Nooo." I patted his chest, still staring at the ring. "Let me do that."

"Silvie, where love and destiny meet, where two hearts beat, so shall the giver adore. Where sacrifice is made, where fire and magic are laid, only one shall be restored. Her name shall be Moyer, with golden fingers and a heart so pure. Her man will bow down, and shall never go hungry before her." He pulled me into his arms. "I wish I could see my father, and thank him for his spell. It's one now etched on my heart."

"One day you will." I held onto him for dear life. "I love you, Guy, and I'll never be parted from you as your father has been."

"I'll never allow it, either. I promise you that." Then he sealed his promise with the deepest kiss, one that stole the last thought from my mind.

Chapter 13

Guy 'ported us into the formal dining room. My sheer happiness gave way to thumping panic in a blink. Four staff members moved around the grand table, aligning stemware and cutlery, making last little changes. "Where is everyone?"

"We're a couple of minutes early." A waiter in black tie stepped forward with a tray and Guy accepted two fluted glasses. Once the man moved away, Guy leaned in, whispering, "I love you."

"I love you too." I rolled my shoulders in an attempt to relax then took one of the glasses Guy offered. The sparkling fruity concoction tingled against my tongue as I sipped. "I can do this."

"Your heart is pure. Of course you can." He led me farther away, where we wouldn't be overheard.

"Wincrest's heart isn't though, Guy. It's as black as can be, and he's a loose cannon waiting to fire."

"I'm here." Faith raced through the engraved oak double doors in a one-shoulder amethyst lace gown. Her lips were pinched, her anxiety clear as she skidded to a stop before us. "Mum's right behind me. She knows everything. Dad doesn't keep secrets from her, not anymore."

"Everything, everything? Kate must hate me then." The secrets I'd kept from both Faith and her. Argh, mind-blowing.

"Silvie." Kate burst into the room then swamped me in layers of fine, pale blue chiffon, her hug fierce. "I've missed you."

"You have?" Okay, maybe she didn't hate me.

"Yes," she murmured, "I felt deceived at first, but then I came to understand. Nothing's ever come in the way of yours and Faith's friendship, and that's the most important part of all. Even now you stand by her side. I love you for it."

"I've missed you too." I hugged her back, my relief enormous. Kate was as easy to love as Faith, and had mothered me as wonderfully as my own mum had.

"Tomorrow we'll talk more." Her brown eyes sparkled, and her long chestnut-brown hair streaked with blond swayed as she nodded. "Come riding with the girls and me. We're still trying to get Faith on a horse, although having you there might help."

Faith groaned. "Or not. I don't like those thingies."

"They're not thingies." I tweaked her nose. "And you're coming since your mother asked so nicely. We stick together."

"We need to set some boundaries on this sticking together deal. Horse riding shouldn't be on it, not when teleportation eliminates my need for them."

"Did someone mention horse riding? I'm up for that." Hope hurried across wearing a figure-hugging gown of royal blue. Another well-dressed young woman followed close behind her. Hope tugged the blond haired woman to her side. "Silvie, meet my aunt, Goldwyn Wincrest. Goldie, Silvie."

Goldie sighed and shook my hand, mumbling, "Another Carver. I can't believe there're two of you. Silas is bad enough on his own."

"She's a Moyer now." Hope nudged Goldie's shoulder. "Be good, okay?"

"I'm just about a saint with how good I've been lately." Goldie extended her hand to me and I shook it. "Alexo has foreseen you're of no immediate harm to us. Although, look after

Guy and steer clear of Dralion business, and we'll get along just fine."

"I can't guarantee a thing." There wasn't a chance I'd steer clear of Dralion business, not now it was mine too.

She snorted. "Yep, you're clearly related to Silas. What is this world coming to?"

"Ladies." Maslin, impressively decked in a navy suit, joined us.

Hope linked her arm through his. "Hey you. What do you think about putting Faith into the mustering team? Then she'd really learn how to ride a horse."

"What?" Faith flicked Hope's arm. "Don't try and turn this conversation back toward me."

"I have to distract Goldie somehow."

Maslin stroked Hope's hand. "Mustering is a great idea. Faith would surely learn to ride if she joined one of the teams. If that's what you'd like, I'll organize it."

Oh, his adoring act was good.

"Enough about the horses." Faith darted a look at the door. "Dad's coming."

"Kate, I've never seen you move so fast." Dralion's Prince Alexo Wincrest, crossed the gleaming black and white diagonal tiles. He strode toward us in inky dress pants, shirt and tailored jacket. Even his tie was as dark as the rest of his clothing. He wrapped an arm around Kate's waist. "You didn't wait for me."

She smiled at him. "Faith said Silvie was here. I haven't seen her in so long."

His penetrating violet gaze clashed with mine. "I watched you and Faith as children through my forethought. Remain as loyal to my daughter as you always have, and we'll never have an issue."

I leaned against Guy, his solid support unwavering. "I'll remain loyal to both your daughters, as they have with me. And as I now do with my mate." I wouldn't let Alexo Wincrest get to me. I had to remain strong tonight. Faith and Hope were depending on me.

"Your enchanter will keep an eye on you." Alexo tipped his blond head toward Guy. "Correct?"

"She'll go nowhere without me." Guy tightened his hand on my hip. "She holds my heart as deeply as she holds the other half of my soul."

"Yes, Guy. We live for our mated one." Alexo brushed a kiss against Kate's cheek. "I fully agree." He glanced over his shoulder. "Nicolas comes."

The healer, suited in black, walked through the doors toward Faith. He lifted her hand and kissed it with a flourish. "Hello, my beauty."

"Are you still sure? I understand if you want to back—"

"I'm sure, Faith. I sense the bond between mates because of its undeniable strength. That shouldn't be taken away, not even because of whom you've chosen."

"You're amazing."

Alexo gripped Nicolas's shoulder. "Your loyalty goes without question, as does my gratitude to both you and Maslin. I don't exactly care for whom my daughters are mated to, but I would never take their choices from them as Donaldo did with me. The bond is too precious."

Kate gasped. "Shh, here comes Donaldo."

Chandeliers dripping in fine crystal swayed as Wincrest and the leading eight filed in. Killian and Abelard's gazes shot toward Faith and Hope. Their lips twisted as Nicolas and Maslin stepped in front of the girls and made a very obvious stand.

Killian marched toward Faith, and Nicolas countered his move until the two stood chest to chest. One fire-breathing dragon tattoo curled up Killian's neck, just visible above his black collar. "What are you doing, Nicolas?" Killian sneered.

"I don't care for your request to court Faith." He slanted his head toward Donaldo. "Your Majesty, Faith and I have been dating, although we haven't spoken of it. It's a fairly new relationship."

Abelard shoved through and heaved in front of Maslin. His single spiked piercing glinted, as did the two swords at his side he slapped his palms over. "Back off. Hope is mine to court."

"You've not been given our liege's permission, and Hope and I have been being seeing each other for months. Make no mistake, she's mine and no one else's."

"It's my decision who will court my granddaughters." Wincrest jerked on the gold cufflinks at his wrists, his imposing height dominating as greatly as his presence. "This is not the right time. Everyone may be seated."

"Yes, I agree." Alexo directed Killian and Abelard to their seats, separating them from the girls, who sat beside Nicolas and Maslin.

Guy steered me toward the chair next to Faith. He opened our link. *"I'll be right across the table from you."* The place settings were named. I didn't want him that far away, not that I had a choice.

I met his gaze as he took his seat. *"Do you think Nicolas and Maslin are up to this?"*

"So much is at stake. Alexo has made it known the girls were born tangled together, arms and legs holding onto each other when the doctor performed the caesarian and delivered them. Neither is the eldest. Both Faith and Hope hold equal positions in line to the throne. Donaldo will want the strongest warriors making a match with them. Two slayers against a healer and one with the water skill." He sighed down our link. *"I don't know which way it'll go."*

Wincrest sat in his throne-like chair at the head of the table, his night-shaded silk shirt a glimmering backdrop for his devious violet eyes. Alexo took the seat to Wincrest's right, Goldie to his left. If Davio and Silas knew where I was right now they'd freak. And if Wincrest ever learnt I was the prince of Peacio's cousin, my life would be forfeit. Out in the blink of an eye.

Faith, at my side, passed me my knife and fork. *"Eat your starter, and tamp down your thoughts. You're broadcasting them to me in a deluge, and I'm already on edge as it is."*

"Sorry." She'd easily catch them with her skill. *"If you could look at Nicolas as adoringly as you can, then that'd make me feel better."*

Nicolas slid his arm along the back of Faith's chair, rested his hand on her bare shoulder. "Faith," he murmured, low enough only she and I heard.

She glanced at him. "Yes."

"As we planned."

"Okay. I need to make Silvie feel better, anyway." She leaned in and kissed his cheek, no hesitation. At the other end of the table, Killian thumped his hands against the table and rattled the plates.

"Enough, Killian." Wincrest rose to his feet. "As much as it's my decision who courts my granddaughters, I will take their wishes into account." He eyed Faith. "It appears you have a preference. If that's the case, I need to hear confirmation of it so we may all enjoy our meal in peace."

"Yes. I prefer Nicolas. He's a healer and so compassionate and kind. I've been drawn to him from the moment we met."

Wincrest switched his gaze to Hope. "And you, my dear?"

Abelard shoved his chair back. "Sire, I've not been given the chance to enjoy her company as Maslin has."

"Settle, Abelard. I will hear what Hope has to say."

Hope gripped Maslin's hand and smiled at him. "I would choose the man I've worked alongside these past two years. Maslin wants the same things as me, and I want him."

"As I want you." Maslin stroked her blond hair.

No way. If Silas ever saw that, Maslin's blood would spill.

Crap, and Nicolas was tucking Faith against his side. Shoot. Davio would bust his gut to get his hands around Nicolas's neck.

Alexo rose. "I applaud the girls' decision, and fully stand behind them."

"I do believe they've chosen well." Wincrest lifted his long stemmed glass and raised it in a toast. "To approved courtships and"—his gaze moved to Guy—"the newly married. My congratulations to you all."

"Here. Here." Guy reached toward me with his glass in hand. *"You truly are the key. Let's seal the toast."*

"Did we just do it? Was that truly Wincrest's acceptance?"

"He loves his granddaughters. We should have factored that into any decision he made."

"Okay, Wincrest might have one redeeming quality, but that's it." I tapped my glass to his as several others at the table clinked their glasses together too. All but Killian and Abelard. No surprises there.

Faith gripped my hand. *"We did it. That's the hardest thing I've ever done. Hold on. Something's happening."* Her eyes glazed over. *"Oh my goodness. Another forewarning."*

Alexo bolted to his feet, his gaze clearing too. "Did you get that, Faith?"

"Gerritt Moyer's on his way, but how, Dad?"

"Divine intervention." He ran to the balcony's glass doors and flung them wide as Gerritt shimmered onto the landing.

Gerritt's clothes dripped, all muddied and ragged. Wincrest joined them, clasped Gerritt's shoulder. "You've escaped?"

"No, Your Majesty, I was freed. Where's my son?"

"Dad?" Guy struggled to his feet. "Is that really you?"

"Yes. I'm back." Gerritt stumbled toward Guy and pulled him into his arms. "I love you."

Holy moly. How was Gerritt back? *"Silas?"* I threw open our link. *"Gerritt Moyer's been released. Would you care to explain?"*

"Hey, I was just going to tell you what happened. Davio felt conflicted about keeping Guy's father locked away. He decided

to make the first move, to ensure Guy understood our working together would not be broken by us. One protector and one warrior at a time, remember?"

"Oh, trust me, Guy already understood that, but, wow. Thank you. Tell Davio I love him, and what's he's done means the world to me." Tears streamed down my cheeks, my relief and happiness too great to withhold. *"I love you too. Tell Davio he won't regret this."*

"I know he won't. Love you."

Guy gripped his father's face between his hands. "How are you free? How is this possible?"

"I was told nothing, just blindfolded, taken from my cell then 'ported. I wasn't sure where to until I scented fresh air and heard gushing water. The guard slid my blindfold free and told me it was my lucky day, that Loveria had granted my freedom."

"Just like that?"

"The guard flashed away, and with my freedom, so did I. The river was right there. I used it to mask my 'porting airstream through to the dome room."

Guy's gaze whizzed to mine, a hundred questions burning within their depths. "Come. Meet my father."

"Silas just told me Davio released your father." I scurried around the table and he wrapped me between him and Gerritt.

"Thank him for me." Guy nuzzled into my hair. *"Amazing. Our spell worked, Silvie. Where love rises strong, where two souls join for one cause, may fire and magic burn and all who bear witness be completely drawn. May hate melt away in the blaze of truth, and may freedom be granted for the man who saw to my birth."* He feathered kisses over the top of my head. *"You and I have to spell together more often. We're a powerhouse when we do."*

"Davio wanted you to know he's committed to working together."

"My commitment will never waver, and now it stands even

more firm." He eased back a bare breath of space. "Dad, meet Silvie, my mate, and the woman I can't live without."

"Nice to meet you, Silvie." Gerritt kissed my cheek. "Welcome to the family. I believe my wife would have wholeheartedly approved of you."

Cheers boomed and echoed around the room.

Wincrest raised his voice above the din. "Welcome home, Gerritt. Let's celebrate your return. This is certainly a night for revelry."

Warriors thumped their feet, and Hope and Faith squealed as they joined in our hug.

My heart overflowed with joy.

Chapter 14

"Guy, you need to lie still so I can sleep. I have school in the morning."

"I can't." He rolled into me, his midnight black hair flopping forward over his brow. "My father's home. He's home."

I grinned as I kissed him. "Yeah, I know, and if you wanna go sleep with him, I don't mind."

"Careful, or I might take you up on that." He tickled my lips with his fingers. "I love you, and I can't wait for the rest of our lives to begin."

"There's a war to end. Never forget that."

He picked up my hand and traced the two bands, his mother's and mine. "Ours will be a journey for sure, and not all smooth sailing, but I promise you this, I'll never leave your side. Not once. Not ever. You're my home, and wherever you are, is where I long to be." His mouth closed over mine, his kiss sending my pulse skyrocketing through the roof.

Oh wow.

A heat built in my veins.

Love, it was hot and all-consuming, and he was all I'd ever dreamed of. Slowly, I pulled back, my breath coming fast. "Give me a minute."

"A minute's too long."

"I have to master some control over my skill and before we get hitched, otherwise I'm going to set fire to something, or everything."

He chuckled. "I'm going to help you with the mastering. I have an idea."

"Okay, your last few have hit the mark. Shoot."

"Once we're married, we could honeymoon on a deserted island in the middle of the South Pacific. There'll be just you, me, the searing heat of the sunshine and a ton of water right on hand." He leaned in. "Sorry, but your minute's up."

Oh, it surely was, and in the next second, he proved just how very much.

Yes. Life was certainly about to get very interesting.

Love these characters and want more?

Don't miss the rest of this spell-binding series from a *New York Times* and *USA Today* Bestselling Author.

To love and protect…across worlds.

Princesses of Myth

Protector, Book One

Warrior, Book Two

Hunter, (Novella – Book 2.5)

Enchanter, Book Three

Healer, Book Four

Chaser, Book Five

JOANNE WADSWORTH

PROTECTOR

Faith and Davio's Story, Book One

WARRIOR

Hope and Silas's Story, Book Two

HEALER

Belle and Nicolas's Story, Book Four

Chaser

Goldie's Story, Book Five

HUNTER

Lieska's Story, Book 2.5 (Novella)

JOANNE WADSWORTH

Joanne Wadsworth is a *New York Times* and *USA Today* Bestselling Author who adores getting lost in the world of romance, no matter what era in time that might be. Hot alpha Highlanders hound her, demanding their stories are told and she's devoted to ensuring they meet their match, whether that be with a feisty lass from the present or far in the past.

Living on a tiny island at the bottom of the world, she calls New Zealand home. Big-dreamer, hoarder of chocolate, and addicted to juicy watermelons since the age of five, she chases after her four energetic children and has her own hunky hubby on the side.

So come and join in all the fun, because this kiwi girl promises to give you her "Hot-Highlander" oath, to bring you a heart-pounding, sexy adventure from the moment you turn the first page. This is where romance meets fantasy and adventure…

To learn more about Joanne and her works, visit:
Website and Blog
http://www.joannewadsworth.com